"Elevate! In the Name of the Law!"

The two hellions whirled in the direction of the
sheriff's voice, guns sliding from their holsters.
Slade took no chances. Weaving and ducking,
he shot with both hands. The sheriff's gun bellowed beside him.

One of the drygulchers crumpled without a
sound. The other also went down, shooting
as he fell. The slugs fanned Slade's face.

From behind the brush a third gun blazed. The
sheriff sank to the ground with a groan. Slade
boomed a shot at the flash and bounded forward—as one of the drygulchers suddenly
raised himself and took deadly aim at the
advancing ranger . . .

DEATH'S CORRAL is a Pyramid Books original

DEATH'S CORRAL

BRADFORD SCOTT

WILDSIDE PRESS

1

ECHO CANYON—the old-timers who had
first passed that way named it. The
name fitted. The acoustics of the narrow gorge walled by
cracked and broken and fissured cliffs were remarkable, even
frightening. A spoken word was tossed to and fro like a ten-
nis ball as precipice called to precipice. A shout evoked a
veritable witches' carnival of howls and wails and bellows in
every conceivable tone. A laugh was answered by shrieks
of fiendish merriment. Even a whisper ran up the rocks in
mysterious murmurs till at last it died away in long-drawn
sighs of sound. While the beat of a horse's speeding irons set
up a nerve-shattering drumroll that vibrated the ears like the
diapason of hammered steel. And a gunshot aroused a spiral-
ling thunderclap that soared to the startled sky.

The Mexicans had another name for the ghastly hole. In
their laconic patois they said, *cementerio*—graveyard.

That name also fitted. For the canyon was a narrow gate-
way from the north to the sinister trail that slithered through
Persimmon Gap on its way to the Rio Grande and Mexico.
Through Echo Canyon the Plains Indians raided into Mexico by way of Comanche Crossing. Wideloopers used it as
a short cut for stolen herds. Under the frown of its crags,
smugglers bartered with buyers. Outlaws, sometimes with
peace officers hot on their trail, found it a convenience.
Its stones were blackened with dried blood, its floor sown
blue with bones. Echo Canyon had known much evil, and
would know more.

So Ranger Walt Slade, sitting on his tall black horse on the
lip of the east wall, who had heard of Echo Canyon and
wondered if its echoes were really as remarkable as they
were claimed to be, gazed into the gloomy depths of the gorge
with interest.

"Shadow," he said to the horse, "I slipped. We should have

taken the north fork of the trail back there to the east; that would doubtless have led us right to the canyon mouth. Why this snake track ran up to the cliff summit, I'm not sure. However, very likely the Indians used this spot as a sort of lookout post—you can see to the north for miles. Then when something promising came into sight, they'd slide down the north slope, which doesn't look very difficult, and be all set for business. So we'll follow their example and hope we don't collect too many scratches."

Shadow snorted equine disgust but did not otherwise comment. Slade chuckled, and continued to gaze into the dark depths of the canyon where the trail which wound through it, nearly three hundred feet below, was but a grayish trace in the gloom.

He was still a bit puzzled about the trail that led to the cliff top. As he said, it had very likely been originally used by Indians, but it showed indubitable indications that a horse or horses had used it quite recently, and frequently. Which was the reason he had turned from the more beaten track which, of course, led to the various ranches to the north, the trail by way of which he had entered the section from the north and east. Well, he had so far been unable to gratify his curiosity. Later he would, in a somewhat startling manner. At the moment he decided the chances were it meant nothing, anyhow. He dismissed the matter from his mind and concentrated on his more immediate surroundings.

Slade made an eye-filling picture as he sat on his magnificent horse in the deep glow of the afternoon sun. Very tall, more than six feet, his wide shoulders and broad chest slimmed down to a lean, sinewy waist, and his face was in keeping with his splendid form. His rather wide mouth, grinquirked at the corners, relieved somewhat the tinge of fierceness evinced by the prominent hawk nose above and the powerful jaw and chin beneath. His pushed-back "J.B.", the broad-brimmed Stetson favored by cowhands, revealed a wide forehead surmounted by crisp thick black hair. The sternly handsome countenance was dominated by black-lashed eyes of a very pale gray, the kind of eyes associated with the intrepid gunfighters of the Old West. They were cold, reckless eyes that nevertheless always seemed to have little devils of laughter lurking in their clear depths, devils that could surge to the front, did occasion warrant, and be anything but laughing.

Thus the man the Mexican *peones* of the Rio Grande

villages named *El Halcón*—The Hawk—"the singingest man in the whole Southwest, with the fastest gunhand," sat and gazed into the murky depths of Echo Canyon, *Cementerio.*

"Well, Shadow—" he began. "What in blazes?"

The canyon had suddenly eructed a booming rumble that got louder and louder, and which Slade identified as the magnified beat of a speeding horse's irons on the rock floor.

"Well!" he exclaimed, "that hole is all that's claimed for it when it comes to kicking up a racket!" He leaned forward, peering.

"Say, that fellow is sure sifting sand," he added.

Another moment and the rider flashed past, to the accompaniment of an outrageous tumult, a vanishing shadow amid the shadows.

But the tumult didn't lessen. It doubled, trebled, quadrupled. Abruptly the canyon exploded a volcanic roar that vibrated the cliff top. Gunfire!

Five more horsemen flickered past. The tense watcher on the cliff could see the reddish flashes. The echoes bawled and bellowed.

Abruptly the shooting stopped. "Got him!" shouted a voice and this was followed by a wild laugh.

"Got him! Got him! Got him!" howled the echoes, with screaming bursts of demoniac mirth.

The uproar ceased as suddenly as it began and there was comparative silence broken only by mysterious mutterings and hissings. Then again the amplified rumbling of hoofs that soon died away to nothingness.

"Let's go, horse," Slade said quietly. "Could be only a sheriff's posse chasing an owlhoot, but somehow I don't think so. I think a snake-blooded killing took place in that hole. Well, we'll try and find out."

It took time to negotiate the slope, for it was grown with thorny chaparral. Shadow collected a few scratches and Slade got a welt on one bronzed cheek where a trailing branch whipped him.

Finally, however, they made it to the level rangeland. A few score yards westerly and the canyon mouth yawned before them. Slade sent his mount into it and the devilish chorus of echoes began afresh. Shadow didn't like the looks of the blasted hole and signified his displeasure by snorting, rolling his eyes, and flattening his ears.

"That row won't hurt you, even though it is hard on the eardrums," Slade reassured him. "Just take it easy and keep your eyes peeled; no telling what we are liable to run into."

He used his own eyes continually, for here, amid the constant uproar of the echoes, his keen hearing was of little use.

But those eyes were the eyes of *El Halcón*, which folks maintained could see around corners and through chunks of mountain.

For perhaps a quarter of a mile he rode slowly, then abruptly reined in.

The dead man lay in the middle of the trail, his arms wide-flung, his glazed eyes staring stonily at the sky. His horse was nowhere in sight. Apparently it had followed the others, or had been led away.

After a quick but all embracing glance at his surroundings, Slade dismounted and approached the body. One look told him the man had been shot to pieces.

"That was no sheriff's posse," he told Shadow. "A posse doesn't gun a man like this and leave him lying. Looks like we barged into something the moment we hit the section. Well, it's in line with the reports that have been coming into Ranger headquarters."

He started to squat beside the body, then abruptly straightened up; the echoes had begun muttering again.

Directly ahead the canyon curved sharply. Slade stood perfectly still beside the body, waiting.

Around the bend bulged two riders. They jerked their mounts to a slithering halt, peering. One let out a shout, "Get him!" Hands flashed to gun butts.

Slade, weaving and ducking, drew and shot, left and right. One of the riders spun from the saddle and thudded on the rock floor. His companion gave a yell, his left arm flapping grotesquely, and lurched to the right. His answering bullet ripped Slade's shirt sleeve. Slade fired again, aiming to cripple, not kill, for he ardently wished to take the fellow alive. But just as he pulled trigger, the other lurched back and caught the slug dead center. He toppled from the hull and lay motionless beside the first. The riderless horses, snorting and blowing, dashed past Slade and up the canyon, setting the wild echoes flying in sober earnest.

Ejecting the spent shells from his guns and replacing them with fresh cartridges, Slade walked forward and gazed down at hardlined countenances blotched and spotted by dissipation. Border scum of the worst sort.

"Now what is this all about?" he asked Shadow. "Did the hellions recognize me as *El Halcón?* Looks sort of that way, unless they were just a pair of mad-dog killers. Well, perhaps we'll get the answer at Sanderson. Hope we find Sheriff Tom Crane in his office; he may know something. We'll pack that poor devil over there to town with us—less than fifteen miles to go and you've packed bodies that way before, so don't start fussing. Fellow looks like a Mexican, doesn't he? A Mexican of all or nearly all Spanish blood. Not a bad-appearing jigger, quite different from these two devils. They'll have to wait till the sheriff sends for them; three carcasses would be a mite too much for you, I'm afraid."

"One's bad enough," Shadow's snort seemed to say. "Let's get going, I'm hungry."

"Take it easy," Slade replied. "I'm not quite finished yet."

He turned out the two dead killers' pockets, discovering nothing he considered significant, just the various trinkets usually carried by range riders, which the pair appeared to be. Had been, rather, for their hands showed no recent marks of rope or branding iron. Each divulged quite a bit of money, which he replaced.

"More than they ever saved from following a cow's tail," was his comment. "I've a notion we did a pretty good chore, here. Well, we'll find out, perhaps in Sanderson. I hope so."

He draped the body of the killers' victim back of the cantle, securing it with his piggin string or short tie rope. Then with a last look at the two owlhoots, for he was very much of the opinion that they *were* owlhoots, he mounted and continued on his way through the eerily resounding gorge.

As he rode, Slade studied the canyon, endeavoring to ascertain the source of the really remarkable echo. Gradually he became convinced that most, if not all of the echoes, were thrown back by the west wall. This was interesting, for the two walls seemed identical in formation.

And as he drew nearer the south mouth of the gorge, the echoes dimmed, became muffled, then ceased altogether. Which was also interesting, he thought, seeing that the configuration of the walls was apparently no different from farther up the canyon.

"Very peculiar," he observed to Shadow. "Now just what is the explanation, I wonder."

Shadow either didn't know or if he did he preferred to keep the knowledge to himself, seeing as the only reply he vouchsafed was a derisive snort.

"Just the same," his rider insisted, "when I get the chance I'm going to do a little investigating."

He rode on, his eyes thoughtful, puzzling over the unusual

phenomenon. After a while he put the matter into the back of his mind for future reference and turned his thoughts to more immediate matters.

2

THE SUN was low in the west when, without suffering mishap, Slade reached the south mouth of the canyon. A mile farther on, he knew, was the east-west trail that led to Sanderson, the railroad town and his destination.

Striking the trail in due time, he rode west at a steady gait, Shadow making light of the double burden he was packing. Slade figured he had something less than a dozen miles still to go. He did not push the horse and it was well past dark when he saw the lights of Sanderson twinkling in the distance.

Sanderson is located in a deep canyon, one wall of which rises over the main street. It had been, and still was, a wild frontier town when Walt Slade rode toward it under the bonfire stars of Texas that seemed to almost brush the cliff tops. It was a repair and division point on the Southern Pacific, with large railroad shops and yards.

Sanderson, founded by "Uncle" Charlie Wilson in the 1880's, had always been wild and wooly, but the arrival of the railroad brought more citizens, some of them not exactly desirable, more saloons, and more trouble. Outlaws roamed the mountains and canyons of the Big Bend country to the southwest and, among other dubious things, trafficked in "wet" herds stolen in Mexico and driven across the Rio Grande, often at the old Comanche Crossing. Nor were they reluctant when it came to rolling Texas cows across into *mañana* land, where there were buyers awaiting them. Stagecoaches and railroad trains were not exempt, nor were banks or other depositories for cash.

"Judge Roy Bean, Law West of the Pecos," owned a saloon there for a time where, as in Langtry, his "own" town, he was wont to dispense justice with a law book in one hand and a six-shooter in the other.

Many of Sanderson's citizens were as colorful as the town's history. The Regan brothers, principals in the story of the "Lost Negro Mine," perhaps the most famous of all the "lost" mines of Texas, had dwelt here for a while. A Negro who worked for them had been sent to round up some stray horses. He returned, not with the horses, but with his pockets full of rocks. The brothers cuffed him for disobedience and fired him, chasing him out of their camp, not realizing until he was gone that the rocks he had found were rich in gold ore. It was said that the Regans spent a fortune trying unsuccessfully to find the missing colored man.

This story and others passed through Walt Slade's mind as he drew near the town. He was familiar with Sanderson and knew where to find the sheriff's office. When he drew rein beside the building, he saw a light burning in the office. He dismounted and entered.

Grizzled old Sheriff Tom Crane glanced up from his desk, inquiringly, stared and jumped to his feet.

"Slade!" he exclaimed. "So McNelty sent me *El Halcón*, the notorious outlaw too smart to get caught! Well, this is better luck than I'd hoped for. How are you, Walt? Man! Am I glad to see you! Sit down, sit down. I've got a pot of coffee steaming. Imagine you're hungry, but we'll have a cup together before hunting something to eat."

"Just a minute, Tom," Slade replied as they shook hands. "I want to show you something my horse is packing."

With the puzzled sheriff following, he led the way to where Shadow stood patiently waiting.

"For the love of Pete!" Crane exploded. "It's a dead man, ain't it?"

"He looks sort of that way to me," Slade returned composedly. "Perhaps you know him."

He raised the dead man's head so Crane could peer at his face. The sheriff did so and uttered a startled exclamation.

"Heck and blazes! He is, was, rather, Rafael Vergara, *Don* Pancho Arista's cart train manager, a sort of field man who contacted the buyers and shippers to the north and east. Walt, this is bad. It's liable to mean big trouble, as if we didn't have trouble enough already. He—"

"Wait," Slade interrupted. "Let's pack him into the office and then, after I've stabled my horse, you can tell me about it. Stable around the corner is still there, I imagine?"

"That's right," said the sheriff. "Old Tomas Cano still runs it; he'll remember you. I'll give you a hand with the carcass."

"No need," Slade replied. Deftly unroping the body, he lifted it with no apparent effort, carried it into the office, and laid it on the floor, straightening the limbs and folding the hands peacefully on the breast.

"Now for my cayuse," he said.

"Okay," replied the sheriff. "Coffee will be ready when you get back.'"

It was but a short walk to the livery stable. The door was opened by an elderly Mexican who peered at his late visitor, then cried out with delight, "*Capitán!* Is it really you?"

"Guess it is," Slade replied smilingly, extending his hand, which the old fellow took diffidently, bowing his white head.

"*El Halcón!* The good, the just, the compassionate, the friend of the lowly," he murmured. "*Capitán,* I am honored. And the beautiful *caballo!* Doubtless he remembers me." Shadow, who allowed no one to touch him without his master's permission, thrust his muzzle into the fearlessly extended hand and blew softly through his nose.

"*Sí,* he remembers," chuckled Tomás. "The stall, the rubdown, and the oats for him. It is the pleasure to care for such a one."

Knowing that all Shadow's wants would be provided for, Slade said goodnight to Tomás and returned to the office, where cups of steaming coffee waited.

For a while he and the sheriff sipped in silence, then Slade rolled a cigarette with the slim fingers of his left hand and suggested, "Now suppose you finish what you started to tell me about *Don* Pancho Arista."

"Well," answered the sheriff, "it's like this. Arista owns a string of carts that ply back and forth between the Rio Grande and here and on to the north and east. Has always had just about a monopoly of the business; been in it for years. But about six months back, John Webb, who owns the Cross W ranch to the north of here, decided to start a line in competition with Arista. I figure Arista didn't pay the competition much mind. But Webb found he had most of the folks tied up in contract and hasn't been doing nearly as well as he'd hoped to, and doesn't like it. He's an old shorthorn type, and Arista is sorta fiery, so they had words. Webb has been making big medicine. Swears he'll run Arista out of business before he's finished with him. Up to tonight, nothing really bad happened. A couple of Arista's carts were burned here in town, and, of course, he blames Webb. I have my doubts that Webb had anything to do with it, but some of his hands who are wild young hellions might have. Anyhow, it didn't serve to ease the tension. Arista growled and grumbled and asked me to try and run down the hellions responsible; didn't ask very nice. I've a notion, though, that he would have forgotten all about it before long.

"But what happened tonight is different. Vergara was his *amigo*, as well as his employee, and Arista will be fit to be hogtied when he learns about it, and of course, he'll blame Webb."

"I see," Slade said thoughtfully. "The making of real trouble."

"And now, suppose you tell me just what happened, and how Vergara came to get killed, if you know," the sheriff suggested.

Slade told him. Crane swore sulphurously. "And you got two of the hellions, eh?" he growled.

"I got a couple of trigger-happy gents who tried to down me," Slade replied. "I can't say that they were members of the bunch who killed Vergara, although I presume they were."

"And they were dressed as cowhands?" Slade nodded.

"But they evidently had not worked at it for quite a while," he added. "Which would tend to rule out Webb's punchers, would it not?"

"Uh-huh," agreed the sheriff, "but it won't rule out the possibility that they were hired gunslingers Webb brought in to do his shooting for him. That's what Arista will say, on that you can bet a hatful of pesos."

"Very likely," Slade conceded. "Now what are you thinking about?" For Crane was muttering under his breath and tugging his mustache.

"I was thinking," he explained, "that Webb is might apt to think, once you're recognized in a few places, that Arista has brought in *El Halcón* to do *his* shooting for him."

"Possibly," Slade admitted with a smile.

"Which puts *you* on a spot," Crane snorted. Slade laughed.

"Won't be the first time," he said cheerfully. Crane snorted again.

"I don't believe you've got a nerve in your body," he complained querulously. "Sometimes I think you enjoy getting shot at."

"I don't mind so long as the slug doesn't connect," Slade replied, still cheerful. "Is Arista a Mexican?"

"Pure blood Spanish-Mexican descent, but born in Texas, as was his father before him," the sheriff answered.

"Texas citizen of at least the second generation," Slade commented. "And Webb, is he an old-timer hereabouts?"

"Oh, sure," said Crane. "The Webb family has owned the big Cross W since a few weeks after Noah landed the Ark, I figure."

"So, two real old-timers on the prod against one another," Slade nodded.

"That's about it, I guess," admitted Crane. "Well, I'll mosey over to Echo Canyon in the morning and pack in those carcasses and put 'em on exhibition. Maybe somebody will recognize the hellions and be able to tell us something about them. Rather too much to hope for though, I reckon. Hungry, ain't you? I know I am; listening to you gab about how you've given some gents their comeuppance always starves me. So let's amble over to the Branding Pen—a new saloon and restaurant in town—and tie onto a surroundin'. Okay?"

"By the way," asked Crane as they headed for the restaurant, "do you figure those two devils recognized you as *El Halcón?*"

"I wouldn't be surprised if they did," Slade admitted. "Looks like the only logical explanation for their going after me like they did. Of course, however, if they were members of the bunch that killed Vergara, they might have figured me a possible witness to the shooting that should be eliminated."

"Could be, but somehow I doubt it," said Crane. "I'm of the opinion they did recognize you as *El Halcón* with a reputation for horning in on good things other hellions have started. That could be the answer, too. Remember, it wasn't to stop a cart war that McNelty sent you here, but to help me clean out a nest of snakes that have been raising heck and shoving a chunk under a corner hereabouts for the last few months."

"We'll take that up later," Slade said, adding, "and it's just possible that there could be a tie-up between the two; I've known such things to happen before. The chance that those two killers recognized me as *El Halcón* causes me to lean to that possibility."

"That loco *El Halcón* business will end up getting you into trouble, one way or another, see if it don't," Crane grumbled.

Which was just what Captain Jim McNelty, the famous Commander of the Border Battalion of the Texas Rangers, more than once told his lieutenant and ace-man.

Because of his habit of working under cover whenever

possible and not revealing his Ranger connections, Walt Slade had built up a singular dual reputation. Those who knew the truth, like Sheriff Tom Crane, maintained vigorously that he was not only the most fearless but also the ablest of the Rangers. Others, including some puzzled sheriffs and marshals, who knew him only as *El Halcón*, a man of dubious reputation with killings to his credit, were wont to insist as vigorously that he was just a blasted outlaw too smart to get caught, so far, but who would eventually get his comeuppance.

The fact that the deception did lay him open to grave personal danger at the hands of some trigger-nervous deputy or other peace officer, to say nothing of professional gunslingers out to enhance their reputation by downing the notorious *El Halcón*, "the fastest gunhand in the whole Southwest," and not above shooting in the back to attain their end, bothered Slade but little. And he pointed out that as *El Halcón* avenues of information were opened to him that would be closed to a known Ranger. Also, that outlaws, thinking him just one of their brand, were apt to grow careless and tip their hands.

What counted most with him was the saying of the Mexican *peones*, "*El Halcón* the good, the compassionate, upon whom rests God's benison."

So Slade went his careless reckless way as *El Halcón*, whenever possible, satisfied with the present, looking back on the past with no regrets, and giving little thought to the future.

3

"THINK ANYBODY will recognize you as a Ranger?" Crane asked as they pushed through the swinging doors.

"I rather doubt it," Slade answered. "I hope not, be better that way." Crane snorted dubiously.

The Branding Pen was big, well-lighted, and noisy. Slade liked the looks of the place with its long and shining bar, lunch counter, tables for leisurely diners, more tables for gamesters. Two roulette wheels whirred, there was a busy faro bank, a dice table, and a full dance-floor. A Mexican orchestra played music he thought was quite good.

"Hardrock Hogan owns it," said the sheriff. "Used to be a cowhand, then turned miner and did some prospecting on the side. Made a pretty good strike and invested the money in this rum hole. Runs a square place and 'pears to be doing rather well."

"And will continue to do so, I venture to presume," Slade commented. "Sanderson will always be a good town, and prosperous, being a division point with the big railroad yards and shops. I've a notion it will grow a mite and tame down as the years pass."

"Sure ain't tame now," grunted Crane. "A natural for owlhoots, and they come from all points of the compass. I feel pretty sure the bunch that's been operating in the section, east, west, north, and south, has headquarters here or near-by."

"Not beyond the realm of possibility," Slade conceded. "You can tell me more about it while we eat," he added as they occupied a table and gave a waiter their order.

"Been making most of their town raids out of my county," said the sheriff. "But everybody 'grees they have their headquarters hereabouts. That's the chief reason I wrote to McNelty for a few Rangers—county lines work to our disadvantage; you can't go bargin' into another gent's bailiwick. Sheriffs are touchy about that, feel that it reflects on their own ability. Don't feel that way about a Ranger.

"The hellions robbed a bank way up at Stockton, another one at Ozona—oh, it was them, all right. Held up the Langtry stage twice. Robbed a train just a few miles to the west of here. Worked that one mighty slick. Had one of their bunch on the train. At the right spot he pulled the signal cord, knew just how to handle it. Engineer stopped to see what the blankety-blank was wrong with his train. The rest of the bunch bulged outa the brush and took over. Blew open the express car, killed the messenger, and made off with better'n thirty thousand dollars. It's a smart outfit, all right, with a jigger with a headful of brains running it."

"Any description of their personal appearance?" Slade asked. Crane shook his head.

"Nothing that's worth a blankety-blank-blank," he replied. "They're always masked with black rags that cover their whole faces. 'Pear to be about average in size, nothing outstanding about any of them. Cashier of the Stockton bank said the hellion that 'peared to be running things spoke well, but not like the average brush popper. Said he didn't 'pear to be very big but was well-built. That's about the best we've got so far, and it ain't much." Slade nodded agreement.

"And the spreads to the north have all been losing stock," the sheriff continued.

"And I haven't been able to clap eyes on any blankety-blank who looks to be a suspect," he concluded morosely.

"And the chances are you won't," Slade remarked. "One might be sitting at the next table and you wouldn't recognize him as such, from his appearance. That's one of the handicaps under which the peace officer labors; outlaws don't look like what outlaws are commonly supposed to look like. And folks who appear to fit the popular conception of what an outlaw is supposed to look like usually are not outlaws. Take that big fellow at the far end of the bar, for example, who glances this way every now and then. With his rather wide, almost reptilian mouth, his narrowed eyes, crooked nose, underslung jaw, and blue jowls he fills the bill perfectly. And I'll wager he isn't one."

"You're darn right he isn't," Crane chuckled. "That's Hardrock Hogan himself, and a more honest man never lived."

"Any more robberies hereabouts?" Slade asked.

"The spreads to the north have all been losing cows," the sheriff repeated.

"Run them to the Rio Grande, I imagine," Slade commented. "By what route, would you say?"

"The way you'd figure them to run 'em is by way of Echo Canyon," Crane answered. "It's a prime short cut to the river, and over to the Big Bend country, too." Slade nodded.

"Looks like by keeping a watch at the south mouth of the canyon you might be able to intercept them," he said. "Nothing can go through that crack in the rocks without being heard coming for a great distance."

"Uh-huh, but the only trouble is it don't work out," grunted the sheriff. "Night after night I kept watch on that infernal hole, and nothing came through. And three different times while I was keeping watch, stock was widelooped and run somewhere. 'Peared to head for Echo Canyon but sure didn't go through it. And they'd have to make a long detour, east or west, for there's no getting cattle over the hills. Twice the hands of spreads that had been robbed were hot on their trail, or thought they was, but they always lost it somewhere along the base of the hills and couldn't pick it up again. The Cross W hands swore they weren't an hour behind the rustlers when they left the spread, but just the same they didn't overtake them."

"And you're sure there's no other way through the hills?" Slade asked.

"Sure for certain," replied Crane. "If they didn't go through Echo Canyon, and they didn't, they'd have to go round the hills to the east or west and that's all there is to it."

"Interesting," Slade commented, his eyes thoughtful.

"And darn irritatin'," Crane growled. "Well, here's our helpin'; let's eat."

A period of busy silence followed. Finally the sheriff pushed back his empty plate with a sigh of satisfaction. Slade ordered more coffee and rolled a cigarette.

"Imagine the carting business is lucrative, is it not?" he observed.

"You're darn right it is," Crane replied. "They're doing all right by themselves, and I wouldn't be surprised if they do a little offhand smuggling on the side, which also helps. Yep, it's a worthwhile business."

"Then doubtless some of the carts at times pack a valuable cargo easily disposed of," Slade pursued. Crane nodded.

"So," the Ranger remarked, "it wouldn't be beyond the realm of possibility that your bunch might make a try for the carts."

"Guess so," agreed Crane, "but it would take considerable

doing to pull it off; would have to be a mighty slick scheme. Those carts are guarded by outriders who are always on their toes. Say, there comes one of my deputies; can use him about now."

He beckoned to the tall young man who had just pushed through the swinging doors. Slade ordered a drink.

The deputy came over and joined them, accepting the drink with thanks.

"Slade, this is Bert Ratcliff," the sheriff introduced. "Bert, when you finish your snort, go try and locate Pancho Arista and bring him here. Tell him it's important."

"Certain," replied Ratcliff. He tossed off his drink, nodded to Slade, and departed.

"Arista has got to know about what happened to Vergara, and the sooner the better," Crane said. "He's going to hit the ceiling, but I hope I can quiet him down. Pretty sure you can."

"I'll try," Slade promised.

Sheriff Crane's brow was furrowed and he kept shooting glances to all parts of the room.

"Trying to spot an outlaw?" Slade asked jokingly.

"You've got me all confused with your talk of outlaws not looking like outlaws," complained the sheriff.

"Well," Slade said, "I've sure known quite a few who didn't. For example, over at El Paso, a few months back, I had a set-to with one that looked anything but an outlaw and yet he was one of the coldest killers I ever contacted. Called himself Juan Covelo, although his real name was Hansen, Gus Hansen. Built up the Covelo myth and had everybody in the section jumpy. Quiet, well-spoken, fine-looking. As Hansen, he ran a respectable saloon and restaurant; as Covelo he robbed and murdered. Seemed to take pleasure in killing. His father was a Scandinavian seaman, his mother the daughter of a Yaqui chief. He inherited his fair complexion, yellow hair and very dark blue eyes from his father. As Covelo, he wore a hooded cloak to hide his yellow hair and make his blue eyes appear black. So everybody was looking for a swarthy, black-haired, black-eyed half Yaqui. Took me quite a while to catch on to him. With the aid of Sheriff Arch Hart of El Paso County, I managed to clean out his bunch, but Covelo gave me the slip. Dived off a cliff into a creek and swam in the clear. And I'm ready to wager that right now he's operating somewhere. No one would think, to look at him and observe his attitude, that he was an outlaw, but he is, one of the worst Texas has ever known.

In fact, there was only one thing about him that might be considered off-color. When something riled him, to employ the expression of one of Hart's deputies, his eyes were like the eyes of a mad cat. Which of course could mean no more than that he had an ungovernable temper."

"And he's unfinished business for you, eh?"

"That's right," Slade conceded.

"Well, by the time you're through with him he'll be 'finished' business, I'll bet on that," declared Crane. "I ain't forgot Veck Sosna, the panhandle owlhoot. *He* was unfinished business, for a while."

"But sometimes I think Covelo is worse than Sosna was—more brains," Slade remarked gloomily. "Oh, well, you can't win 'em all."

"Never heard of you losin' any," chuckled the sheriff. "Hello! Bert worked fast. Here he comes with Arista."

Pancho Arista was a strikingly handsome man. Tall, broad-shouldered, he had black hair streaked with gray, piercing black eyes, and a firm but kindly mouth. His eyes widened slightly as they rested on Slade's face, but he acknowledged the sheriff's introduction with a courtly bow. When he spoke it was in colloquial English without a trace of accent.

"Understand you have something to tell me, Tom," he said. "What's on your mind?"

"Sit down, Pancho," the sheriff replied. "I'm scairt I've got bad news for you. No sense in beating about the bush—Rafael Vergara was killed today."

Arista's eyes widened, he looked dazed.

"Killed!" he repeated. "Where . . . why . . . how. . . ."

The sheriff gestured to Slade. "You tell him, Walt," he suggested.

Slade did so briefly, but omitting no detail. Arista's face flushed darkly, his eyes glared.

"The Cross W hellions!" he spat. "Could have been nobody else! I'll—"

"Mr. Arista!" Slade interrupted. The carter jumped in his chair at the change of his voice. "Mr. Arista, it is not commendable for a man of your standing in the community to make wild and unfounded charges. No matter what you may think because you have had a difference with the Cross W, there is not one iota of proof that the Cross W had anything to do with Vergara's killing; and unless those bodies are recognized as former members of the outfit, or some unexpected development occurs, there will still be no proof of guilt against the Cross W."

"But if not the Cross W, who?" countered Arista. "I have no enemies capable of such a deed."

"Vergara was killed, not you," Slade pointed out. "Vergara may have had enemies unbeknownst to you. It is seldom, no matter how closely one may be associated with another, that one knows all the details of the other's private life. There are many ways in which a man may make enemies. Sometimes because of a business deal in which the other party feels he has been taken unfair advantage of. Sometimes through a difference of personal opinion, or a misunderstood act. Mr. Arista, I would like to ask you a question. Answer or not, as you choose: did Vergara possibly carry a large sum of money?"

Arista hesitated and glanced at the sheriff, who nodded.

"It is possible that he did," he admitted. "He rode to Stockton to contact certain buyers and it is not illogical to believe that he made some collections."

"I see," Slade nodded. "And the chances are he would have packed the money in his saddle pouches. And, as I said, his horse was nowhere in evidence. So robbery must not be ruled out as a motive. This, I gather, would tend to eliminate the Cross W outfit as suspects."

"You make a good case for Webb and his hellions," Arista sighed. "But I fear I'll have difficulty altering my opinion."

"That's your privilege, but to voice your opinion without a foundation of fact is an abuse of that privilege," Slade instantly retorted.

Arista looked bewildered and apparently at a loss about how to reply. The sheriff created a diversion.

"Like to take a look at what's left of poor Vergara?" he asked.

"Yes, I would," Arista replied, evidently glad of the chance to end a conversation in the course of which his position was becoming more and more untenable.

"I'll stay here and talk with Bert, if you don't mind," Slade said to Crane. He knew very well that Arista was anxious to speak with the sheriff alone and decided to provide him with the opportunity.

"Okay," said Crane. "See you when we get back—we won't be gone long."

Outside, Arista turned to the sheriff. "Know who we've been talking with?" he asked.

"Yep," Crane answered. "Name's Slade, as I told you—Walt Slade."

"And he has another name," Arista remarked meaningly, "*El Halcón;* I recognized him at once."

"Guess that's so," Crane admitted.

"There are people who say he's an outlaw," Arista snapped.

"That so?" the sheriff returned cheerfully. "Ever see a reward notice for him?"

"No, nor anybody else," Arista exclaimed exasperatedly. "They say he's too blasted smart to ever get caught. He's got a lot of killings to his credit."

"To his *credit* is right," replied Crane. "Like the two devils he did for today."

"How do we know he's telling a straight story about the killing of Vergara?" Arista demanded.

"Because *he* told it," Crane replied, with finality. Arista threw out his hands in an expressive gesture.

"I give up," he said. "You always seem to know what you're talking about when it comes to people. I hope you're not making a mistake this time."

"I am not," the sheriff stated. "And Pancho, I'll tell you something. Walt Slade is a mighty good man to have for you, and a mighty bad one to have against you. Right now I believe he's for you, so don't do or say anything that might cause him to change his attitude."

"All right," Arista said resignedly. "I'll tighten the latigo on my jaw and keep my thoughts to myself."

"A darn good notion," agreed Crane. "By the way, I believe your cook is a Mexican, ain't he?"

"He is," Arista answered. "I never forget that my forebears came from Mexico and I like to provide opportunity where possible for the people from south of the Rio Grande. As you know, I have quite a few Mexicans in my employ. Why did you ask?"

"Because I want you to ask your old cook about *El Halcón* and listen to what he has to tell you," Crane replied. "He's pretty apt to know of *El Halcón,* and what he has to tell you may surprise you a mite. Okay, here we are."

A moment later, Arista gazed sadly at the dead face of his business associate and friend.

"He was a good man," he said. "This shouldn't have happened to him. I suppose an inquest will be held."

"Yep, I'll get in touch with Doc Cooper, the coroner, and we'll hold one after we pack in those other two bodies," Crane said.

"I'll look up the undertaker—I think he's playing cards over at the Regan House bar—and arrange to have the body prepared for a decent burial," Arista remarked. "Poor Ver-gara left no relatives to my knowledge. May drop in at the Branding Pen a little later, if you figure to be there."

"Chances are I will be for a while," Crane replied. "Be seeing you."

Arista hurried off on his sorrowful errand. The sheriff headed for the Branding Pen at a leisurely pace.

4

MEANWHILE IN the saloon, Bert, the young deputy, had proven talkative and thoroughly conversant with conditions in the section. Slade found his remarks interesting and let him ramble on. He noted that Hardrock Hogan, the owner, was eyeing them speculatively. After a bit, he strolled over to the table. Bert performed the introductions and Slade invited Hogan to have a chair.

"Something happened?" he asked as he motioned to the waiter to bring drinks. "I saw Sheriff Crane and Arista have their heads together."

Bert glanced at Slade. "Any reason why I shouldn't tell him?" he asked.

"None that I can think of," the Ranger replied. "He's bound to hear about it eventually, and he might as well get the straight story while he's at it."

Bert proceeded to relate Slade's account of the happening, vividly and true as to detail. When he paused, old Hardrock reached a big paw across the table to Slade.

"Son, you did a good chore, a mighty good chore," he declared. "Betcha those two sidewinders were part of the bunch that's been making trouble hereabouts of late. And Arista blames the Cross W? Rats! Those young hellions are good at getting into ruckuses and starting a fight at the drop of a hat, but when it comes to chasin' a man and shootin' him in the back, I don't believe it. Old John Webb is a salty *hombre* and ready to pull on you if you're standin' up to him, but when your back is turned you're plumb safe. Arista wouldn't shoot a man in the back, either, so he had oughta give the other feller credit for being as square as he is. But when a feller gets his mad up he just nacherly ain't got any brains that are in workin' order."

Slade smiled and didn't argue the point. There was truth

in the old saloonkeeper's homely philosophy, and shrewd
common sense. He regarded Hardrock Hogan as something
of a character, which he was.

Although it was past midnight, the Branding Pen was
still going strong. Even stronger, in fact. The bar was crowded,
as was the dance-floor. All the gaming tables were occupied
and at several Slade decided the stakes were rather steep.
He noted that there were quite a few Mexicans, well-dressed
young fellows, and wondered if they were members of
Pancho Arista's carting outfit, deciding that they very likely
were. Cowhands and railroaders were in the majority, however, and some gentlemen whose antecedents and present
status, Slade felt, were dubious.

Hardrock ordered another drink for Slade and Bert and
stood up.

"Mind if I tell the boys what happened?" he asked of
Slade.

"No reason why you shouldn't," the Ranger replied. "And
you might pass the word that when he brings in those two
bodies tomorrow, Sheriff Crane would like to have the folks
look them over on the chance they might be recognized by
somebody."

"I'll do that," Hardrock promised and returned to the end
of the bar, where he engaged a constantly augmented crowd
in conversation.

As Hardrock continued to speak, Slade noted that the
young Mexicans and several equally young Texans dressed
as cowhands were gathering in a tight group, talking together with compressed lips and frowning brows. Bert noticed the direction of his gaze and answered an unspoken
question.

"The Mexicans are some of Arista's cart drivers, the
Texans his outriders," Bert said. "Reckon they ain't feeling
very happy over what happened. Vergara was a good man
to work with and was popular with the carters and riders.
Could be trouble in here before the night is over."

Slade was inclined to agree and watched the group closely.

"Oh, good gosh!" Bert suddenly exclaimed. "Here comes
the Cross W bunch; must have been holed up someplace
else. Now look out!"

The newcomers, seven in number, were young, swagger-
ing, and boisterous and appeared the worse for wear from
having looked upon the wine when it was red or some other
color. They made their way to the bar not far from where

DEATH'S CORRAL • 27

the carters stood and ordered drinks. Now Slade watched both groups.

Nobody, except Walt Slade, seemed to know just how the fight started. Later, the carters swore they didn't start it. The cowboys maintained just as vigorously that they didn't start it. Anyhow, somebody hit somebody and the ruckus was on, to the accompaniment of shouts, curses, screams from the dance-floor girls, soothing yells from the bartenders. Tables were overturned, chairs smashed, bottles and glasses broken. It was a wild melee of hitting, wrestling, kicking, and gouging.

"Keep out of it," Slade snapped to Bert. "They won't do one another much damage and Hardrock and his floor men will soon break it up."

Bert, who had started to rise, settled back in his chair.

Slade, whose eyes were everywhere, saw the three men edging swiftly toward the swinging doors. He saw their eyes glint in his direction. Two barged through the doors. The third whirled toward him, his hand streaking to his holster. Slade went sideways out of his chair, drew and shot in a single ripple of motion. There was a howl of pain and a gun clattered to the floor. Its owner dived for the outside. Slade blasted three more slugs into the swinging doors and bounded across the room, gun ready for instant action.

But there were excited and bewildered men in his way, an overturned table and a smashed chair. By the time he reached the door and peered cautiously out, there was nobody in sight. He turned back to the rising tumult of the saloon.

The fighting had stopped for the moment but seemed likely to resume at any instant. Slade's great voice rolled in thunder through the room, striking all to silence.

"Stop it! We've had enough foolishness for one night!" The muzzle of his cocked Colt gestured to the carters and the cowhands.

"You fellows get back to the bar and behave yourselves," he told them in tones like steel grinding on ice. "Do you understand?"

Under the threat of that rock-steady muzzle, with the terrible eyes of *El Halcón* behind it, they understood. Both groups, muttering and growling but making no further hostile move, shuffled to the bar. Slade holstered his gun, returned to the table, and began rolling a cigarette. Bert gazed at him, and the young deputy appeared slightly dazed.

"That hellion you winged made a try for you, didn't he," he stated rather than asked.

"He did," Slade replied, finishing his brain tablet without spilling a crumb of tobacco and touching a match to it. "Guess he was a mite slow, though."

"He didn't 'pear slow to me," Bert declared. "But *you* made him look slow as a snail climbing a slick log. Gentlemen, hush! Now I believe it."

"Believe what?" Slade asked.

" 'The fastest gunhand in the whole Southwest,' " Bert quoted. "Yep, I was sorta wonderin', but I ain't anymore. Gentl-l-lmen, hush!"

Slade smiled. "Go over there and see if you can find his iron," he directed. "I think it's on the floor somewhere close to the door."

Bert did so, returning a moment later with the dry-gulcher's gun, or what was left of it, one butt plate being missing and the lock smashed by Slade's bullet.

"Blood spots on the floor, too," he announced. "Reckon you took part of his hand off."

"I thought I winged him, not seriously, however, from the way he skalleyhooted," Slade said as he examined the damaged gun.

Hardrock Hogan came over to the table; his face was serious.

"Mr. Slade, it looks like you made some enemies today," he said as he settled his ponderous bulk in a chair.

"Possibly," *El Halcón* conceded.

"I saw what happened," Hardrock said. "Happened to look toward the door right at that minute. Do you figure that fight was staged as a cover-up?"

"It was," Slade replied, "but not by the carters or the Cross W bunch. I saw one of those sidewinders hit one of the Cross W hands from behind. He naturally figured it was one of the carters and swung on the one nearest. I didn't realize what it meant, at first, thinking it was just an over-zealous *amigo* of the carters perhaps resenting something that was said. But when the three of them headed for the door once the ruckus was under way, I thought it looked a mite funny and watched them."

Hardrock shook his head in wordless admiration. "I think you should have another drink," he said. "I'll send one over before I help the boys clean up that mess of busted furniture. I oughta make the hellions pay for it, but I won't."

"I think I'd prefer a cup of coffee, thank you," Slade answered.

Hardrock snorted. "Okay, okay," he said. "If I was in your place right now, I'd hanker for a double snort to stop me shakin'."

He lumbered off to the kitchen, still wagging his big head. Bert chuckled.

"I watched you roll that cigarette," he remarked. "You sure weren't doing any shaking I could spot. Haven't you any nerves at all? Right now I'm still jumpy as a rabbit in a hounddog's mouth. Here comes Crane."

The sheriff came hurrying across the room, his face mirroring concern.

"I'd stopped at Stampler's place for a minute," he explained. "Heard there was trouble over here and a shooting. Knew darn well you were mixed up in it some way. What happened?"

Slade told him. The sheriff swore. "Figure it was somebody with a grudge against *El Halcón?*"

"Could be, of course, but somehow I don't think so," Slade replied. "Remember, there were five men chasing Vergara. I met two men riding the other way and presume they were part of the bunch that killed Vergara. For some reason two returned to the canyon, perhaps to get rid of the body, or possibly 'discover' it. If so, that would leave three unaccounted for. I feel that the three continued to town. There's just a chance that the three who attempted to drygulch me are the identical three. After listening to Hardrock tell the story of what happened in the canyon, they may have decided that I should be eliminated. Just conjecture, of course, but that's the way I'm inclined to view the incident."

"Think you would recognize those three horned toads if you happened to see them again?" Crane asked.

"I would," Slade answered. "However, I'm of the notion that they'll steer clear of me for a while, realizing that I *would* very likely recognize them."

"Or wait for you up some dark alley," Crane returned meaningly.

"Possibly," Slade smiled. "The moral then being, keep out of dark alleys."

"You won't," snorted the sheriff. "You'll likely go prowlin' 'em. That would be more your style."

Slade laughed and changed the subject.

"The boys over at the bar appear to have quieted down somewhat," he commented.

"I imagine they did after you spoke a gentle word to them," the sheriff agreed dryly.

"Uh-huh, plumb gentle," chuckled Bert. "I jumped half outa my skin. Nearly scared the pants off me, even though I hadn't done anything wrong. I never heard such a voice!"

"Wait till you hear him sing sometime and you'll say that double," observed Crane. "Here comes Arista."

The cart owner appeared worried as he approached the table. "Heard there was trouble here," he said. "Did my boys start something?"

"No," Slade told him. "Nor did the cowhands, intentionally; it was just a mistake." Arista looked relieved.

"I've a notion that gent with a bullet hole through his hand figures it was a darn bad mistake," remarked Crane and proceeded to regale Arista with an account of what happened.

"And you think, Mr. Slade, that those three men were part of the bunch that killed Vergara?" Arista asked when the sheriff paused.

"Not impossible that they were," Slade replied. "And," he added, his gaze hard on the other's face, "if so, it is an example of what happens when honest men get on the prod against one another, each blaming the other for anything off-color that occurs, and providing opportunity for the lawless to operate."

"You may be right," Arista sighed. "But," he added bitterly, "I don't see why Webb should adopt the attitude he holds. I did not resent his entering into the carting trade in competition with me. So far as I was concerned, he was welcome to any business he could get."

Slade refrained from mentioning that it was his inability to get the business he'd hoped for that caused Webb to paw sand, for there was truth in what the carter said. He resolved to have a talk with John Webb at the earliest opportunity.

Arista glanced toward the bar. "I think I'll go over and have a talk with my boys," he announced.

"A good idea," Slade applauded. "Tell them not to start any trouble, and, Tom, it might also be a good idea for you to have a little powwow with the Cross W bunch."

"I will," the sheriff said grimly. "I don't calc'late to have any corpse and cartridge session in this town if I can prevent it, and I've a notion I can."

Slade was inclined to agree; Sheriff Crane was known to be a cold proposition. He leaned back comfortably in his chair, told the waiter to bring more coffee, then rolled a cigarette.

As he watched Arista mingling with his men, Crane with the cowhands, Slade felt he had averted trouble for the time being at least; but he was dubious as to the future. There was no doubt but that Pancho Arista deeply resented Webb's attitude, and he had a fiery temper. It would take little to set him off.

"You sure have whipped the Old Man and Arista into line," chuckled Bert, the deputy. "They both do just what you tell them to and don't arg'fy."

"I just suggest," Slade smiled.

"Uh-huh, like the business end of a six-shooter suggests," said Bert.

Which caused *El Halcón* to smile again. Bert's manner of expressing himself was refreshing.

A little later, Crane and Arista returned to the table. "I'm going to bed," said the latter. "I'm dog-tired. See you tomorrow, Mr. Slade. Later today, rather; it's long past midnight."

"And I think I'll follow your example," Slade replied. "Guess I can get a room at the Regan House, Tom?"

"Sure you can," Crane assured him. "They've always got vacancies. Let's go. I'll knock off a few hours myself and get an early start after those carcasses. Old coots like me don't need much sleep. Come along, Bert, time you was in bed, too."

5

In a comfortable room at the Regan House, named for the Regan brothers of Lost Negro Mine fame, Slade slept soundly till mid morning. After cleaning up and shaving, he tied onto some breakfast at the Branding Pen and then repaired to the sheriff's office.

Sheriff Crane had gotten an early start, all right, and in less than an hour he appeared with the bodies, which he laid out on the office floor for inspection.

Soon citizens began filing in for a look at them, but one and all shook their heads. Never saw 'em before was the general expression that was monotonously repeated until two of the Cross W cowboys who had been at the Branding Pen the night before put in an appearance. They gazed at the dead faces, peered close, exchanged glances and muttered together in inaudible tones. With a glance at Slade they hurried out, heads close together.

Slade noted their curious actions but said nothing. Only, the concentration furrow between his black brows deepened, a sure sign that *El Halcón* was doing some hard thinking. He glanced at Crane who apparently had not noticed the incident.

An hour passed, then abruptly the door was filled by a huge man with gray-streaked hair, hot blue eyes, a stubborn chin, and a tight mouth. His manner was aggressive, almost pugnacious.

"Hello, John," the sheriff greeted. "Walt, this is John Webb who owns the Cross W spread. "John, I want you to know Walt Slade, who gave those two hellions their comeuppance."

"Howdy," Webb acknowledged the introduction in a harsh and deep voice. He stuck out a huge and hairy paw. His grip was hard, almost to the verge of being offensive, but when their hands fell apart, there were white circles around his fingers. He wrung his hand and glowered at Slade with grudging admiration.

"First feller I ever met who could out-grup me," he rumbled. "Where the hell did you come from?"

"Your designation of the general locality is erroneous," *El Halcón* replied smilingly. Webb blinked, stared, and apparently was at a loss as to how to answer, and decided not to.

"I want to look at those carcasses," he growled to Crane.

The sheriff led the way to the back office where the bodies were laid out, Slade sauntering along behind, his eyes hard on old John's face.

Webb bent over, peered, bent closer, peered again.

"What in blazes!" he roared. "Say, I've seen this bigger one. The hellion rode for me about three months back. For four or five weeks, then asked for his pay and trailed his twine. Never saw him again, until today. A good worker, but sorta grouchy. Never mixed much with the boys. I don't think he ever went to town with them. Used to take rides by himself durin' his off hours. Well, if this don't take the hide off the barn door! I suppose Arista will blame me for Vergara's killing?"

"He was inclined to, but I've a notion Slade talked him out of it," said Crane. Webb shot the Ranger a puzzled look.

At that moment, Arista himself entered the office. The two men stiffened, glared, their fingers twitching.

"Gentlemen!" Slade said quietly.

The tension eased as both relaxed. "I'm goin' over to the Brandin' Pen for a snort," Webb growled and stalked out.

The sheriff turned to Slade.

"Well, what do you think?" he asked.

"I think that fellow," Slade replied, gesturing to the corpse, "took those rides to familiarize himself with the area. I would say he was planted with the Cross W to learn conditions and to spot cows for widelooping. Logical to think so."

"Wouldn't be surprised if you're right," agreed Crane. In a few words he acquainted Arista with the latest development. The carter looked dubious but did not comment.

"I think I could stand a drink," he said. "Come along, Mr. Slade, and share one with me?" Slade nodded and they left the office together.

They had just descended the steps when a cowhand rode around the near-by corner, leading a saddled and bridled horse.

"Another one of the Cross W bunch," Arista grumbled.

Abruptly his face darkened, he peered with out-thrust neck and gave a yell of rage. "That's Vergara's horse!" His hand streaked to his left armpit.

But Slade got his wrist before he could trigger the gun he had drawn.

"Have you gone completely loco?" the Ranger demanded.

"Let me go!" stormed Arista, struggling frantically to free his arm. "Let me go! I'll kill the—" His voice rose in a scream of pain as *El Halcón's* terrible grip ground his wrist bones together. The gun fell to the ground.

"Have you gone loco?" Slade repeated. "That would have been cold-blooded murder if you had gone through with it. Behave yourself!"

"Don't!" gasped Arista, his face beaded with sweat, his eyes bulging. "Please don't! You'll break my arm! Please!"

"Will you behave yourself if I let you go?" Slade asked, his voice quiet, musical, as he eased his grip a little.

"Yes! Yes!" Arista panted. Slade let his hand fall and approached the cowboy who was looking white and scared.

"Much obliged, feller," he mumbled. "I thought I was a goner."

"You came very nearly being one," Slade said grimly. "Where did you get that horse?"

"We found him on our south pasture with the rig all askew and tryin' to graze with the bit in his mouth," the puncher explained. "I was bringing him in to turn him over to the sheriff."

Slade speculated the young fellow and believed he was telling the truth.

"Anything in the saddle pouches?" he asked casually.

"Just some duds," the other replied. "We went through 'em thinkin' maybe we could find something that might tell us who he belonged to."

Slade nodded. He believed the puncher was still telling the truth.

"Take the critter to the sheriff," he said. "Come on, Arista."

For a few minutes they walked in silence, then Slade remarked, "Sounded like a straight story, don't you think?"

"Yes, it did," Arista admitted. "And I wish to thank you for what you did. I completely lost control of myself when I saw that horse."

"It would be a good idea for you and Webb both to tighten the latigos on your tempers," Slade admonished. "I can't understand how you haven't gotten into serious trouble before now from flying off the handle that way."

"Just luck, I guess," sighed Arista. "So that outlaw killer once rode for Webb, eh?"

"So Webb said," Slade replied. Arista's brows drew together.

"I wonder," he remarked reflectively, "could it have been that bunch burned my carts?"

"We might venture to presume it was, although we have no proof it was so," Slade equivocated.

"And that fellow rode for Webb, by his own admission," Arista observed, still reflective. Slade was silent.

"But why should the bunch do such a thing on their own accord, from which they could not hope to profit?" Arista continued.

"They, or somebody, might profit if you and Webb had a corpse and cartridge session and did for each other," Slade pointed out grimly. "I gather that carting is a lucrative business."

"I never thought of that," Arista admitted, his face thoughtful. "But—" he left the remark unfinished, glancing sideways at his companion.

Again Slade was silent, for he knew that Arista was still dubious concerning John Webb. In fact, he himself had not made up his mind where Webb was concerned, anymore than he had altogether reached a decision relative to Arista. Webb's ready admission that the dead outlaw had ridden for him might seem to absolve him from complicity, but not necessarily so. Certainly he was shrewd enough to realize that not only his own hands but punchers of other outfits would recognize the man as one who had once worked for him, and that he could hardly do otherwise than admit the fact.

And the two punchers who beat a hurried retreat after a glance at the bodies. Slade was convinced at the time of the incident that they had recognized either one or both of the dead men, but chose not to say so at the moment. Possibly they preferred to wait and learn their employer's reaction before speaking out. Which of course could mean nothing; but then again, it could mean a great deal. Why the reluctance to admit the dead outlaw had been a former working companion? That could be interpreted in more than one way.

No, Webb was not altogether in the clear. He was undoubtedly an obstreperous old shorthorn, accustomed to having his own way, not above riding roughshod over the rights of others if it pleased him to do so. Such a man, feeling that he was a law unto himself, sometimes went too far; Slade had encountered such incidents. Also, there was another angle to consider. More than once, honest cattlemen, and others, had hired questionable characters to do their fighting for them, sometimes to protect their interests, with such characters almost inevitably getting out of hand. Could be the case here, where either Webb and Arista, or perhaps both, were concerned.

They reached the Branding Pen. Arista hesitated.

"Think it will be all right for me to go in with Webb there?" he asked.

"It will be," Slade replied decisively, and meant it. He'd had enough of the shenanigans of the sod-pawing pair and was in no mood to put up with more. If they started a row, they'd have it finished for them in a manner they wouldn't enjoy.

Arista seemed to sense what was passing through Slade's mind, for he closed his lips and followed the Ranger into the saloon.

John Webb was at the bar, mingling with several of his hands. There were none of the carters present. Doubtless they were working. Slade and Arista sat down at a table and ordered drinks. Webb glanced in their direction but did not approach.

Arista made a random remark or two while waiting for their order to be filled, but soon fell silent, for Slade's answers were distraught.

In fact, *El Halcón* was busy with his own thoughts and the problem that confronted him as a Texas Ranger. There was no doubt but that a capable and ruthless outfit was operating in the section. Presumably it was independent of the rival carting interests, but the truth of that last was still to be ascertained. Perhaps robbery, nothing more, was the motive for Rafael Vergara's murder, for Slade still believed the young Cross W cowhand's statement that nothing of value was found in the saddle pouches of Vergara's straying horse.

One thing puzzled Slade. How the devil did the horse reach John Webb's south pasture which, he gathered from the sheriff, was some distance north and east of the north mouth of Echo Canyon. It was hardly conceivable that it had wandered clear around the hills to reach the pasture. And it undoubtedly had fled or been led through the south mouth of the gorge. Looked like it might have been led back through the canyon sometime during the night. Which would seem to indicate that it was "planted" on Webb's pasture for some reason or other.

A deliberate attempt to cast suspicion on the Cross W outfit? Not beyond the realm of possibility, the purpose being to heighten the friction between Webb and Arista.

But who? And why? Slade didn't have the answer to either question, and wished he had. He dismissed the matter from his mind for the time being, smiled at Arista, and rolled a cigarette.

A few minutes later Sheriff Crane entered. He waved at Slade and joined Webb at the bar. For some time he conversed with the rancher then sauntered over to the table and sat down.

"Webb's heard the *El Halcón* yarn and asked me if Arista brought you in to do his shooting for him," he announced. "I told him the notion was just so much sheep dip, but I'm scairt he's still wonderin' a mite."

Arista chuckled. "Last night," he said, "I was wondering for a while if Webb had brought him in to do *his* shooting for him, but I've changed my mind. I figure he doesn't hire out to anybody."

"You're darn right," grunted Crane. "When Walt does any shooting', it's his own notion, not somebody else's. Take yesterday and last night for example. Which reminds me, the inquest will be held in twenty minutes and we'd better be rattlin' our hocks. If we're late, Doc Cooper is liable to throw us into the calaboose for contempt of court. Come on, Walt; come on, Arista. I reckon you'll want to be there, too."

The inquest was brief. The coroner's jury's verdict also brief, and to the point. Rafael Vergara met his death at the hands of parties unknown. The sheriff was directed to run down the devils as quickly as possible. The two drygulchers got just what was coming to them. Slade was commended for doing a good chore on the pair and urged to bring in some more. Court adjourned to the Branding Pen for a drink.

Webb and his hands were still present but apparently tending strictly to their own business and peaceful enough.

"I figure Walt sorta subdued the young hellions last night," Crane chuckled. "Reckon they don't want no part of him. And old John don't look as uppity as usual."

"More likely, he realizes what a lot of people are thinking," Slade said. "Even the coroner's jury gave me the impression that they were just a mite dubious about that 'parties' unknown verdict. I've a notion Webb has always held his comb rather high, and that doesn't set well with folks. There was never a truer saying than 'As ye sow, so shall ye reap.' I wouldn't be surprised if there are those who are not exactly displeased to see him all of a sudden on the defensive, as it were."

"Guess that's so," Crane conceded. Arista nodded emphatic agreement. And, human nature being what it is, Slade felt that the carter rather enjoyed Webb's predicament, even though there might be doubt in his mind that the Cross W had anything to do with Vergara's killing. And he was not at all sure just what Arista really did believe. He was fairly confident that he had sown seeds of doubt in the carter's mind, but with no guarantee that they would flourish and burgeon.

Arista glanced at the clock. "I'll have to get back to my office," he announced. "A lot of work to do. Got a cart train coming up from Boquillas. Should arrive in Marathon later tomorrow evening, by way of the Comanche Trail through Persimmon Gap and then come on to Sanderson the next day."

"Valuable shipment?" Slade asked casually.

"Very," Arista replied. "Goods from Mexico, and money in payment for goods shipped south. I'm not worried about it, though. A picked crew of my very best men handling it; it'll get through all right."

Slade nodded thoughtfully. Sheriff Crane shot him a keen glance but did not comment.

After Arista departed, Crane turned to the Ranger. "Well, what's on your mind?" he asked.

"Tom," Slade answered slowly, "I'm going to play a hunch. Nothing to lose and possibly something to gain."

"I knew it," sighed the sheriff. "I know that look. Well, your hunches, as you call them, usually work out, based on straight thinking as they are. Be taking a little ride, eh? Hadn't I better come along?" Slade shook his head.

"I think I can handle the chore better by myself," he said. "Besides, it'll be out of your bailiwick."

"When it happens another gun might come in handy, any bailiwick is my bailiwick," growled Crane.

"I know that," Slade agreed, "but this will be in the nature of a scouting trip and I figure I can handle it."

The sheriff snorted and didn't look impressed.

———— 6

SLADE WENT to bed early and slept soundly for several hours. Midnight, however, found him in the saddle and riding west toward Marathon. On a rise he pulled up and studied the back track for a while. Satisfied that he was not followed, he continued on his way.

It was fifty miles to Marathon and, the Comanche trail, but Slade, thoroughly familiar with the Big Bend country and its environs, knew of a little used trail that would halve the distance, striking the Comanche some miles south of Marathon. So a few miles west of Sanderson he turned south by west and rode on through the velvet hush of the night.

Only the clicking of Shadow's speeding irons, the whistle of an owl, the yipping of coyotes and the lonely, hauntingly beautiful plaint of a hunting wolf broke the silence. It seemed to Slade that he swung in limitless space between two eternities, with the crest of a rise ahead the threshold of the nameless worlds.

A night of peace and beauty, the wild and rugged beauty of the wastelands, claiming him for its own.

The great clock in the sky wheeled westward. The stars turned from gold to silver, dwindled to needle points of steel piercing the robe of night, vanished. The east glowed rose and gold and pulsing scarlet. Objects lost their vague opaqueness, resolved to forms and shapes with edges clear-cut. A shaft of light shot to the zenith, fell to earth in a shower of molten bronze. The sun arose in majesty, and it was day.

Now he was well into the grim fastness of the Big Bend, following the general route traversed by Spaniards in their exploration of the most forbidding part of New Spain. For the tide of Spanish exploration split upon the rock formed by the Big Bend country and ebbed and flowed along either side, marked by tragedy as starvation, thirst, savage beasts, and savage men took their toll.

He glanced about and got his bearings, for now he was riding the old Comanche Trail. Far to the south loomed Santiago Peak, used by the Indians as a lookout. Sentinel Peak, sixty miles across the Rio Grande, was also in sight, a landmark in the Big Bend, another Indian lookout post. To the left of Sentinel soared the pointed crag of Needle Peak.

Soon the twin black peaks of Dove Mountain appeared, with Cupola Peak to the south.

An hour later found Shadow toiling into Persimmon Gap, through which pass in the Santiago Range runs the Comanche Trail blazed by raiding Indians.

From the gap Slade had an excellent view of the distant Chisos Mountains. High, multicolored, and hazy, they bulked in a serrated mass on the horizon to the southwest. Blue, red, purple, and yellow, ever-changing as the angle of the sunlight moved, they were awe-inspiring in their rugged vividness.

At the southern lip of the pass, Slade drew rein and sat gazing southward, trying to estimate how far distant the carts should be at the moment. If they had kept to their schedule and hoped to reach Marathon by nightfall, they wouldn't be so very far ahead. The train had doubtless broken camp at dawn and the carts, each drawn by four horses, would maintain a steady pace at fair speed.

"Maybe we're just chasing our tail through the brush, but somehow, horse, I don't think so," he told Shadow. "I've got a hunch somebody is going to make a try for that train. How? Haven't the slightest idea. It'll have to be a smooth move, all right, with the outriders on the job. Arista said they are an efficient bunch, and I expect he knows what he's talking about. Well, we'll see. The big idea is how to go about it."

For some little time he sat studying the terrain ahead. Thoroughly familiar with the Comanche Trail, he knew that sometimes it ran between rocky cliffs, at other times in the shadow of long slopes, often brush-grown. Sometimes the way on either side was clear, so that the outriders could keep their distance from the train and spot anything approaching it. At others, when the growth encroached on the track, they would have to move in close.

"And if anything is tried, I'd say it will be at such a spot," he said. "Let's go, horse."

Descending from the pass, he rode the trail for a while. Then, where the track ran between two slopes that were not very high, he sent Shadow up the right-hand sag, reaching its crest, which was thinly brush grown, without mishap.

"I think there's enough growth to conceal us effectively," he observed. "Especially as all eyes are apt to be focused lower down. Now we're between three and four hundred yards from the trail and can see ahead for quite a ways. Which is all to the good. Take it easy and keep your eyes open. I happen to know that this trail-growth prevails for quite a few miles, and I've a feeling that if something is tried it will be along here somewhere."

Shadow didn't argue the point and they moseyed on, Slade constantly studying his surroundings, especially the winding trail ahead.

He had made several miles of slow progress when he spotted the train, far to the south, a disjointed worm crawling steadily northward. His unusually keen eyesight noted that the outriders had been forced to move in close because of the encroaching growth, pacing their horses at the edge of the track. He continued on his way. When he met the train, he would turn and ride parallel to it, always keeping out of sight. And constantly he studied the terrain ahead.

Fairly swiftly he closed the distance between his position and that of the carts, which now were visible in detail. And abruptly he saw something that aroused his interest. Perhaps half a mile from where the train moved, less than that from his own changing position, the growth, tall and thick, edged even closer to the gradually curving trail. And the tops of the tall growth were moving gently.

"Now what the devil?" he wondered aloud. "There's not a breath of wind blowing. What's causing those upper branches to sway? Looks like something is brushing against the trunks, just as a horse would forcing its way through that tangle. Speed up a little, feller, this calls for a mite of investigation. But surely nobody not completely terrapin-brained would try to stage a drygulching under such circumstances, with the outriders on the alert as they certainly are. A little more, horse, this is getting darn interesting."

Shadow quickened his pace, Slade keeping him well behind the thin screening of growth, confident he would not be noticed from the trail. Now he was opposite the growth of mysterious movement, the train something like six hundred yards to the south and moving steadily. Slade pulled to a halt, his gaze shifting from the growth to the carts and back.

On came the carts, rolling steadily. They were bunched together; the lead horses of one had their noses over the tailgate of the vehicle ahead.

"Somebody's using bad judgment," the Ranger muttered. "Anything happen to set one team of horses off and it would spread to the others."

Now the lead cart was directly opposite where he sat his horse and but a few yards from where the closer growth began at the beginning of the curve. Slade estimated the distance. A little over three hundred yards from his position to the trail. Excellent shooting distance for the eyes of *El Halcón* and his high-power Winchester, did it come to that.

Suddenly Slade's astonished eyes saw a gray streamer rise from the brush. With incredible swiftness it changed to a black column, a rolling cloud. Almost under the noses of the lead horses shot up a wall of flame. They screamed, surged back, whirled to flee. Over went the lead cart. The one behind followed suit. The terrified horses tore free from the harness and went charging back along the line, spreading panic. Two more carts were overturned. Chaos, utter and complete, ensued. Outriders, carters, and horses were a howling, screaming, demoralized mob.

Slade sent Shadow surging forward beyond the very edge of the crest growth.

From the brush below streamed a dozen or more masked men, shooting as they came. Slade saw an outrider fall, another. His Winchester fairly leaped from the saddle boot gushing flame and smoke.

One of the raiders threw up his arms and slumped to the ground. The rifle spoke again. A second masked man went head over heels like a plugged rabbit.

Slade was in plain sight from the trail and answering slugs stormed about him, some uncomfortably close. He did not move back but continued to give battle to the outlaws. A third raider reeled sideways but remained on his feet.

But now the cart guards, given a moment of respite and a bit of encouragement, had recovered from their panic and were blazing away wholeheartedly. A third owlhoot fell, and another. The remainder, evidently at a word of command, whirled and streaked back into the brush.

Another moment and the tops of the growth waved wildly. Slade followed the tossing branches with slugs till the magazine was empty. A few minutes later, as he shoved fresh cartridges into the Winchester, he saw the outlaws break for cover far to the south and go racing down the trail.

The carters and the outriders were shouting and waving to him. Slade gestured understanding and sent Shadow down the slope. As he drew near the trail, a reek of kerosene stung his nostrils.

So that was how the devils did it! Soaked big heaps of brush and the surrounding growth with oil and set a match to it at just the right moment. A highly ingenious scheme. Slade felt he had never heard of its equal. And had he not persistently followed his seemingly loco hunch, it would have succeeded.

"Feller, you were the answer to a scared cowpoke's prayer," shouted a fresh-faced young Texan, one of the outriders. "Where the devil did you come from, and how did you catch on so quick?"

"I saw what was going on from up on the crest and I figured I'd better take a hand," Slade replied. The guard and his companions were too excited and grateful to think to ask what he was doing up there.

"Anybody hurt?" he asked.

"Nothing worth making a fuss over except two of the boys who won't ever be hurt again," the cowboy replied. "Anyhow, between you and us the count is twice over evened. Four of the sidewinders done for, and one was wobbling when he went into the brush."

Slade found a couple of bullet wounds, not serious, that he treated with medicants from his saddle pouches. Several carters had suffered cuts and bruises during the melee, nothing of any consequence.

The fire had died down rapidly. There were a few flickers here and there amid the chaparral, but the growth was too green to burn readily and there was no danger of a bad brush fire.

"Now you'd better catch the horses and right those overturned carts and be on your way," Slade told the carters and guards. "I don't think there'll be any more excitement today." He signalled to the young Texan.

"Let's see what we bagged," he suggested. Together they turned to the dead raiders.

"Got 'em all dead center," chuckled the guard. "Never knew what hit 'em. Say! Ain't those the darndest-looking masks you ever saw? Sorta remind me of pictures I saw back in school of the king's axman in the old days, who chopped off heads of fellers the king didn't like. Went all covered up so nobody could know who he was. Axman might be the king himself, for all anybody knew. Maybe he was sometimes and worked out on some jigger he had a bad grudge against."

The masks *were* peculiar. Not only did they cover the entire face but the back of the head and most of the neck as well. Slade stared at them, his brows drawing together. The blasted things struck a chord of memory.

7

THERE WAS nothing particularly outstanding about the faces revealed. The young guard 'lowed they were hard-looking characters and Slade did not contradict him. With the guard's help, he methodically went through the dead men's pockets, discovering nothing of consequence, so far as *El Halcón* could see, except a surprisingly large sum of money.

"Divide it up among the boys," he told the guard.

"But how about you?" asked the other. "I figure you earned it all."

Slade smilingly shook his head. The guard shot him a look, shrugged, and did not protest further, doubtless realizing it would be a waste of time.

Order quickly replaced chaos. The horses, which had not run far, were caught, the harness mended, the overturned carts righted. One with a damaged wheel was abandoned, its load apportioned among the others. The bodies of the two murdered guards were tenderly placed in room made for them, the carcasses of the outlaws unceremoniously dumped amid the loads. A search had failed to discover the horses they rode; evidently they had followed the others. Slade approached the Mexican carters who bowed reverently. He spoke to them in flawless Spanish, whereupon they bobbed and grinned and looked very pleased.

The young Texan, whose name was Clyde Hopper and who was captain of the guard, noted this, but did not comment. The fire had burned down to wisps and smolders, so the train got under way. The horses eyed the burned-over stretch suspiciously and snorted protest, but moved ahead. Soon the long train was again rolling on toward Persimmon Gap and Marathon.

"Going to be late when we reach town, but we'll make it,

thanks to you," Hopper said to Slade. "By the way, do you happen to know our boss, Pancho Arista?"

"Yes, I know him," Slade admitted.

"He'll sure have plenty to say to you," Hopper declared. "The loss of this train would have hit him hard. A lot of *dinero* represented by those loads and the money tucked away among them. Yep, he'll have plenty to say, and he won't forget you." He paused, looked contemplative.

"The boss and old John Webb, who owns the Cross W spread—I rode for him once—have had some trouble," he remarked.

"I know," Slade replied, "but," he added smilingly, "I think it would be a bit illogical to blame Webb for what happened today, don't you?"

"Yep, I reckon it would," Hopper conceded. "Old John is a proddy gent, but somehow I can't see him hiring a bunch of sidewinders to rob and murder. Of course, though, fellers have been known to hire tough bunches to sorta protect their interests and then have them slide out of the loop and start hell raisin' on their own."

That Slade was forced to admit was so, although he rather doubted it was the case in this particular instance.

"I've a notion that John Webb is the sort to do his own fighting and not call on outside assistance," he observed.

"He always struck me that way," Hopper conceded.

The train rolled through Persimmon Gap and down the opposite slope to the level ground. After a while Slade said to Hopper, "Here's where I turn off and head for Sanderson. What happened was in Brewster County, so turn the bodies over to the sheriff and tell him about what took place. Tell him that if he wishes me to be present at the inquest he will doubtless hold, to get in touch with Sheriff Crane at Sanderson. Go ahead, I don't anticipate any more trouble for you today."

"Okay," answered Hopper. "And much obliged again for everything. See you in Sanderson."

With the lower edge of the sun touching the horizon, Slade drew rein beside a small stream where grass grew.

"About time we put on the nosebag," he told the horse. Removing the rig so Shadow could graze and roll, he dumped a helping of oats from his saddle pouch. From the pouches he took a store of staple provisions, his small skillet, and a little flat bucket. Kindling a fire, he got busy preparing supper. Soon bacon and eggs were sizzling in the pan, coffee bubbling in the bucket. The pouches also produced a loaf of bread.

He ate his simple meal with relish, cleaned up, and stretched out beside the fire with a cigarette. He'd give Shadow another hour of rest before resuming his journey. Meanwhile he gave himself over to thought, pondering the day's development; he couldn't get the peculiar masks worn by the raiding owlhoots out of his mind. Juan Covelo, the El Paso outlaw who escaped him some months before, had worn a hooded cloak to hide his yellow hair. "The "headsman" mask would serve the same purpose. He had all along expected Covelo to start operating somewhere, sooner or later, and wondered if this was it.

Could be. If so, he had a problem on his hands to tax the courage and ingenuity of even *El Halcón*. Covelo was no ordinary brush-poppin' owlhoot; he has brains. Brains plus stark daring and utter ruthlessness. It seemed absurd to think that Covelo planned to run both Pancho Arista and John Webb out of the carting business and take over the lucrative trade himself, but Slade felt he wouldn't put it past the cunning devil. As Gus Hansen, respectable saloon and restaurant owner, he had terrorized the El Paso section for quite a while and had proven his ability to take advantage of any opportunity that offered. Could be Covelo here. The killing of Rafael Vergara and the raid on the cart train showed the Covelo touch.

Be that as it might, the indubitable fact remained that somebody was operating in the section, operating shrewdly and with daring and ingenuity. And if it did happen to be Covelo, there was no telling what the resourceful scoundrel might accomplish were he not stopped.

Meanwhile an interesting conversation had taken place between young Clyde Hopper, the captain of the carting guards, and an old Mexican driver.

"Pete," asked Hopper, "who is that big feller? You boys seemed to know him."

"He is *El Halcón*," replied the driver.

"*El Halcón?*" Hooper repeated. "That means The Hawk, don't it?"

"*Sí*. He is *El Halcón*, the good, the compassionate. He is a strange man, *Capitán*. Where there is trouble, *El Halcón* appears, and the trouble departs."

"The troublemakers today sure departed, all right," Hopper agreed dryly. "Didn't seem to want any part of him."

"They were wise," said the driver. "In the hour of his wrath he is terrible, but he is good."

"Said he knows the boss," Hopper observed. "I'll have to ask Arista about him; chances are he'll know."

"Many are the stories told of *El Halcón*," the driver remarked. "But only those that tell of the good he does are true."

"I can well believe that," said Hopper.

After the fire had burned down to ashes, Slade got the rig on Shadow and continued to Sanderson, arriving at the canyon town shortly after midnight. He cared for his horse and then repaired to the sheriff's office where a light burned. As he expected, Sheriff Crane, fortified with his pipe and a pot of coffee, was waiting for him.

"Well, did the hunch pan out?" the sheriff asked, pouring a cup.

"Quite satisfactorily," Slade replied and reviewed the day's happenings. Crane shook his head.

"I wish I knew how the devil you do it," he sighed. "How come you figured they'd make a try for that train?"

"I recall mentioning to you that I wouldn't be surprised if a try was made for one of the trains," Slade answered. "And when Arista told me the one rolling up from Boquillas would pack a very valuable cargo, which I suppose was generally known, it seemed to me that it was reasonable to believe that a try might be made for that one. On the surface it appeared that an attempt on the heavily guarded train would be sheer lunacy. So I knew that if an attempt was made, it would be something daring, audacious, and ingenious. Well, it was, all right. Took me completely by surprise. If I'd caught on a little sooner I might have been able to save those poor devils of guards."

"I don't see how," said the sheriff.

"If when I first noticed the tops of the chaparral swaying I had poured slugs into the growth I might have thrown the hellions off balance," Slade replied. "I just didn't catch on quickly enough. Well, I suppose it's impossible to think of everything in time."

"I figure you did enough," declared Crane. "You saved the rest of them and the drivers. I've a notion it would otherwise have been wholesale murder."

"Possibly," Slade admitted, thinking of Juan Covelo and his method of operating.

Ouside sounded hurried footsteps. A moment later Pancho

Arista burst into the office waving a sheet of yellow paper. "Just got a wire from Clyde Hopper, the cart guard captain," he announced. "I can't make head or tail of it. Hopper's a good worker and capable, but I always thought he was a mite loco. Guess he's cracked up at last. Read this!"

He thrust the telegram under the sheriff's nose.

Despite the grim import of the message, Sheriff Crane roared with laughter as he read it.

Patrick and McHenry killed. Loads safe. Vive El Halcón.

"I don't see anything funny about it," snorted Arista. "Two good men killed! And what the devil does that *Vive El Halcón* mean?"

"You tell him," the sheriff said to Slade.

The Ranger proceeded to do so. Arista swore fluently in two languages, then solemnly shook hands.

"No use trying to thank you for what you did," he said. "I would like to express my appreciation in a more practical and fitting manner."

But Slade, understanding what he meant, shook his head smilingly but with finality.

"I only wish I had been able to do more," he said. "As I was telling Tom, if I'd just caught on a little sooner I might have saved the two guards."

"No man could have done more," Arista declared with decision. "You certainly have no reason to blame yourself on that score."

Slade fingered the telegram. "It would seem Mr. Hopper has a sense of humor," he commented. "He struck me as being an able and intelligent young man."

"Oh, he's all of that," conceded Arista, "but I think macabre describes the quality of his sense of humor."

"Whatever the devil that means," grunted the sheriff. "I knew a feller over in Alpine named Mack Kober, but there wasn't anything funny about him."

"Grisly might also be fittingly descriptive," Slade smiled. "But young fellows like Hopper, who look death in the eye with frequency, are apt to regard it lightly. Familiarity breeds contempt."

"Guess that's so," conceded Arista, "but as you grow older, you accord greater respect to the 'Grim Reaper,' feeling his cold breath on your neck. Yes, grisly is also appropriate."

"Grizzly!" snorted the sheriff. "Now I suppose you're talking about bears. Trying to keep up with what you fellers are sayin', without a dictionary handy, is a chore."

Slade laughed, and changed the subject.

"I directed Hopper to inform the sheriff of Brewster County of what happened and to tell him that if he wished me present at the inquest to get in touch with you, Tom."

"Okay, I'll take care of it," Crane promised. "Now what?"

"Now I crave a session of ear pounding," Slade replied. "Had very little sleep last night, and it's been a busy day. See you tomorrow, Mr. Arista."

Slade went to bed, to dream of Macabre leading his skeletons, all of whom wore black "headsman" masks that covered the back of the skull, to the grave in the dance of death.

8

HE CHUCKLED over the dream the following morning as he walked through the brilliant sunshine to the Branding Pen and breakfast; dreams were amusing things.

But there was nothing amusing about the possibility that Juan Covelo really was operating in the section. That was a deadly serious matter, as Slade well knew, and might well be deadly, period, for him. For if Covelo was in the section, he must know that *El Halcón* was again on his trail. *El Halcón,* the man he had sworn to kill at the first opportunity.

Well, he hadn't had much luck so far, and perhaps his lack of luck would hold. Slade believed it would and sat down to a table in a cheerful frame of mind.

A hearty breakfast with plenty of steaming coffee made him feel even more cheerful. A walk in the sunshine and a few words with Shadow also helped.

"We're not doing too bad," he told the big black. "With a mite of help, we've been able to account for seven of the devils, and I've a notion an eighth isn't feeling any too good right now, from the way he wobbled when he skalley-hooted into the brush. So stop your grumbling and take it easy. Nothing to be pessimistic about."

Shadow refused to comment, so Slade tweaked his ear and went in search of Sheriff Crane, whom he found busy at his desk.

"Got a wire from Sheriff Traynor over at Marathon," he announced as the Ranger entered. "Says he'd like to have us both at the inquest tomorrow evening at seven o'clock. Why he wants me I'll be hanged if I know, but that's what he said."

"Perhaps to advise him as to how to deal with notorious *El Halcón,*" Slade smiled. Crane snorted.

"Darned old terrapin-brain," he grumbled, apropos of the Brewster County peace officer. "Shall we go by train? It's quicker."

"If you don't mind, I'd prefer to ride," Slade replied. "Never can tell when we might need our cayuses."

"That's right," Crane agreed.

"If we start early, we can make it without difficulty," Slade added. "And the weather is fine."

"Okay, we'll trail our twine right after daybreak," nodded Crane.

"Expect the carts will roll in sometime today," Slade observed.

"Will be a long and hard pull, covering that distance in one day," the sheriff commented.

"Yes, but they can do it if they keep moving," Slade said. "I imagine Hopper will be anxious to get those loads and the money to Sanderson as quickly as possible. I doubt if he'd chance a night camp on the way."

Slade was right. The cart train did arrive, long after dark. He was sitting at a table in the Branding Pen, after enjoying a late dinner, when Clyde Hopper entered, glanced about, and hurried to the table.

"Figured I might find you here. Got something to tell you," he announced.

"Yes?" Slade replied interrogatorily, waving him to a chair and beckoning a waiter.

"Yes," Hopper said, sitting down. "I couldn't deliver that message to the sheriff over there for you. We took the bodies to the sheriff's office, as you told us to. Wasn't anybody around but the door wasn't locked so we packed 'em inside and laid 'em out on the floor. The boys made camp and headed for something to eat. I went looking for the sheriff. Didn't find him, but did find a deputy I know. Deputy said that Traynor was down at Costolon, by the Rio Grande, on some business. Wouldn't be back until late tomorrow at the earliest. Deputy promised to relay the message to him soon as he got back. I figured you'd ought to know about it."

"I'm very glad you told me," Slade replied, his eyes very thoughtful. "And you're sure he said the sheriff wouldn't be back until tomorrow?"

"That's what the deputy said, and I reckon he ought to know," Hopper answered. "I know he hadn't come back this morning. Deputy said he'd look after the bodies but couldn't decide what to do about an inquest until Sheriff

Traynor got back. Said he reckoned Traynor would get in touch with you as soon as he got back."

Slade sat silent for a moment, while Hopper addressed himself to his drink and motioned the waiter for refills for both of them.

Abruptly he turned to face the guard captain. "Clyde," he said, "will you do me a favor?"

"Huh!" exclaimed Hopper. "Is there anything I could refuse you, after what you did for us down on the trail? What is it?"

"Just this," Slade explained, "don't mention what you just told me to anybody; I have a reason for asking."

"If you've got a reason, I reckon it's a good one," Hopper answered cheerfully. "Okay, I'll keep the latigo tight on my jaw."

Slade asked a question, "Did anybody overhear what the deputy told you relative to the sheriff's absence from Marathon?"

"Why, I reckon they did," Hopper replied, looking puzzled. "I found him at a bar and there were quite a few fellers around who could have heard if they were listening. Didn't know there was any reason for keeping it secret and didn't ask him to keep his voice down. Yep, I reckon others heard what he said, all right."

"And how about your boys, did they know about it?" Slade pursued. Hopper shook his head.

"I didn't discuss it with them," he said, "so I reckon they don't know about it. Say, what's going on, anyhow?"

"I'll tell you later," Slade answered. "And thank you again for bringing me the word so promptly."

"Glad I did," said Hopper. "I'm going to have something to eat—been quite a while since I tied onto a surrounding."

"Good trip?" Slade asked by way of a diversion.

"Fine," the guard captain replied. "We just kept rolling along. I was going to make town tonight or fail up. I sent one of the boys to tell the boss I'd be here. Reckon he'll want to check the load, even if it is late."

While Hopper ate, Slade sat smoking and sipping coffee, and thinking hard, contemplating just what use he should make of the information he had received. Rather surprising information, everything considered. Might well be highly important, even mean the difference between life and death for himself and Tom Crane. Finally he resolved not to mention what he had learned to the sheriff, for the time being at least.

For he was formulating a plan, a plan that called for

absolute secrecy were it to possibly succeed. He debated whether or not to try and dissuade the sheriff from accompanying him on the trip, but, rather reluctantly, dismissed the idea as not feasible. And after all, if his conclusions were correct, the capable old peace officer might well come in very handy.

It was a daring plan, something like walking into a den of grizzly bears and punching them on the nose. But Slade believed there was a chance that it would work if his estimate of the situation was not erroneous, and it might rid the section of a pest once and for all.

So he decided to put it into effect and was fairly sanguine as to the outcome.

He had no fear that Crane would do any talking out of turn did he know what was in the wind; but his attitude might give the thing away were somebody keeping close tabs on them in town, which Slade believed might be the case.

Arista arrived before Hopper finished his meal and was treated to a vivid account of what happened on the trail south of Persimmon Gap, stressing the part Slade played.

"So you stood out in the open and shot it out with them, eh?" he scolded. "I knew darn well you weren't giving us half the story. To hear you tell it, it was just a lucky break with no danger to yourself. Glad you came across with a true yarn, Hopper. Leave it to him and he'll never get the credit due him."

"Well, he gets the credit from us fellers," said Hopper. "If it wasn't for him, I wouldn't be here telling you about it, and that goes for the rest of the boys. Loads all okay, and the money, too. I left Miguel and Sebastian watching over them with a couple sawed-off shotguns."

"They had those scatterguns trained on me when I was ten yards away, before they recognized me," Arista answered. "Yes, everything is okay. *Vive El Halcón!*"

It was Hopper's turn to bellow laughter. "I thought that was a good one when I wrote it," he chuckled.

"I didn't see much humor in it last night, but things look a bit different today," Arista admitted, with a smile. "Well, I'll get back to checking loads. Waiter, fill 'em up again for my *amigos*."

A little later the carters and the guards filed in and business picked up.

Slade watched for a while, then said goodnight to Hopper who joined his companions at the bar, and retired to his room; a few hours of sleep were in order.

He and the sheriff left town at daybreak. Slade rode casually as the miles flowed back under the horses' speeding irons, apparently relaxed and carefree, conversing with his companion. But always his eyes were searching the terrain ahead, noting and evaluating the movements of birds on the wing, little animals in the brush, the drift of cloud shadows through the chaparral, his keen ears listening for any alien sound.

The miles flowed back, the sun crossed the zenith and slid down the long slant of the western sky, and nothing happened. They were now less than a dozen miles from Marathon and Slade began to wonder if perhaps he had been mistaken in the conclusions he drew.

Then suddenly from the brush ahead that encroached on the trail, and at the beginning of a bend, darted a javelina pig, squealing angrily. It sped across the trail, still squealing, and vanished into the brush on the far side.

"Hold it!" Slade said, in low tones as he reined Shadow in. "Keep your voice down!"

"What—what—" began the startled sheriff.

"Quiet!" Slade interrupted. "I don't like the way old bristle-back acted. Something sure set him off—something scared him, and javelinas don't scare easy. Listen, now. Ease your horse into the chaparral, as quietly as possible, out of sight from the trail. Okay, this is far enough."

"Won't you please tell me what's up?" breathed Crane. "Did you see something?"

"No," Slade replied, "but that little hog evidently did. Now I'll tell you what I didn't before. That message you received was not from Sheriff Chet Traynor. Somebody sent it to lure us onto this trail today; I'll explain everything later. I've a notion that right ahead somebody, more likely several somebodies, are holed up waiting for us to show. I could be wrong, but I don't believe I am, and we can't afford to take chances."

"What are we going to do?" whispered the sheriff.

"If we work it right and you don't mind taking a chance, we may be able to turn the tables on the devils and give *them* a nice surprise," Slade replied.

"I'll take a chance," Crane answered grimly. "Be glad of the chance to take one. You give the orders and I'll toddle right along with you."

"Will your horse stand, and keep quiet?" Slade asked.

"Yep, he's well-trained," said Crane.

"All right, then," the Ranger explained. "we'll leave the

horses here and slide ahead through the brush, keeping back from the trail. If I'm correct in my surmise, the sidewinders will be at the edge of the growth, watching the bend in the trail. Stay right behind me and for Pete's sake don't make a noise or *we'll* be the ones to get the surprise. All ready? Let's go!"

9

SLOWLY AND in utter silence, Slade led
the way, bending under branches, care-
fully stepping over tufts of low growth, pausing often to
peer and listen. The sheriff, familiar with such work, trailed
after him, equally silent.

They covered at least fifty yards, keeping back from the
edge of the growth. Abruptly Slade halted. To his keen ears
had come a low mutter of voices almost opposite from
where they stood scarce daring to breathe. Slade eased forward a step, then another, and sighted the quarry, two masked
men standing at the edge of the growth, their eyes fixed on
the trail. They were not more than ten feet distant.

Slade hesitated; they would be justified in downing the
murderous devils where they stood. But he was a Texas
Ranger, bound by the stern code of the Rangers.

"We'll have to give them a chance to surrender," he
breathed to Crane. "You do the talking."

The sheriff's voice rang out. "Elevate! In the name of the
law! You're covered!"

The pair jumped, whirled in the direction of the sound,
guns sliding from their holsters. Slade took no chances and,
weaving and ducking, shot with both hands. The sheriff's gun
bellowed beside him.

One of the drygulchers crumpled without a sound. The
other also went down, shooting as he fell. The slugs fanned
Slade's face. He bounded forward as the outlaw flattened out.

From a few yards down the line of brush a third gun
blazed. The sheriff sank to the ground with a groan. Slade
boomed a shot at the flash and leaped forward. Through a
rift in the growth he caught a glimpse of a man swinging onto
the back of a horse, a slender, broad-shouldered man, a
black mask covering his head and neck. Slade threw up his

Colt, then slewed sideways and down. One of the "dead" drygulchers had raised himself on an elbow and was taking deliberate aim. His bullet ripped the brim of Slade's hat. Then he pitched forward to lie still as the Ranger's answering slugs hammered his body. Slade scrambled to his feet, glaring at the motionless form.

"Blast you! you'll stay dead this time, but you gave the hellion the start he needed," he growled disgustedly, listening to the beat of fast hoofs on the trail. He hesitated an instant, half inclined to get Shadow and give pursuit, but refrained; the sheriff needed attention.

With a final swift glance at the motionless drygulchers, he turned and hastened to where Crane was groaning and rolling his head from side to side. Slade knelt beside him, anxiously. To his great relief, he spotted only a trickle of blood from a slight cut just above the sheriff's left temple. The bullet had barely grazed him, knocking him out with the shock. A moment later, with Slade's assistance, he sat up, holding his head in his hands.

"How you feel?" Slade asked.

"Okay, except my head's spinnin'," Crane mumbled, and shook that member vigorously. "Did you get the blasted vinegarroons?"

"We got two of them, but the third got away," Slade replied. "And I'm willing to swear he's the big he-wolf of the pack. I'd recognize his build and the set of his shoulders anywhere. The hellion always seems to get a break, one way or another. Think you can stand?"

"Give me a hand and I think I can," Crane replied. A moment later he was on his feet, weaving slightly but his strength was quickly returning.

"I'm all right now," he said. "Let's see what we bagged."

They stripped off the masks and gazed at the dead faces.

"Guess you're right when you say there ain't nothing about owlhoots' looks to make 'em stand out from honest folks," the sheriff grumbled. "This pair looks just like ordinary cowpokes."

He proceeded to turn out the pockets, discovering nothing of interest save a good deal of money which he pocketed.

"Turn it over to Chet Traynor to help pay for planting them," he said. "What shall we do with the carcasses?"

"I think we'll find their horses somewhere near," Slade replied. "We'll pack them to town and turn them over to Traynor."

The horses were discovered not far off, tethered to branches.

They were good-looking animals and docile. Slade studied the brands.

"Blotted," was his verdict. "Somebody did a very neat job with a running iron; you'd have to take the hides off and look at the insides to read the original burns. Would very likely mean nothing, anyhow. Horses can be bought, traded, or stolen and turn up a long ways from where they were foaled."

The bodies were quickly roped into place across the saddles, and the burdened horses led to where Shadow and the sheriff's mount waited.

"Let's go," Slade said. "Be dark before we reach Marathon at this rate. How's your head feel?"

"Okay," Crane answered. "Ache has about stopped and I'm seeing clear again. Was close, though. Another inch to the right and it would have been curtains. It was the one who got away that plugged me, wasn't it?"

"That's right," Slade replied. "He holed up away from the other two, which was characteristic of him. I just about had sights lined with him when that other devil raised up and did his best to take me with him. That was close, too. If I hadn't spotted him when I did, he would have gotten me dead center. Oh, well, it didn't work out too bad, everything considered."

"You're darn right," agreed Crane. "Now as we jog along, suppose you give me the lowdown on how you caught on to what was due to happen."

Slade did so. "Juan Covelo has a hair-trigger mind and instantly recognizes opportunity," he concluded. "Either he or one of his bunch overheard the deputy tell Hopper that Sheriff Traynor wouldn't get back from Costolon until late today. Covelo saw his chance; sent that fake wire and set his neat little trap for us. If it hadn't been for Hopper telling me what he did, it might well have worked, for we would not have been suspecting anything out of the ordinary. Well, it didn't, thanks largely to that pig."

"Oh, I've a notion you would have spotted the hellions, anyhow, pig or no pig, the way you must have been keeping watch," Crane declared with conviction. "The blankety-blanks!"

Dusk was falling when they reached Marathon and headed for the sheriff's office with their grim cargo. / crowd, constantly augmented by new arrivals, trailed a   them, exclaiming and chattering.

Sheriff Chet Traynor, big, burly, and jovial, aroused by the commotion, stepped out the door as they drew rein.

"What in blazes!" he exclaimed. His glance fell on Slade's face and he started visibly. He let out a bellow, "Jim!"

A deputy hurried out to join him. "Keep an eye on the horses and those carcasses," Traynor ordered. "Keep everybody out. You two fellers come in and give an account of yourselves."

Once inside the office, he shut the door and turned to Slade.

"So the notorious outlaw is still gunnin' down honest citizens, eh?" he chuckled. "Well, you brought a duly elected peace officer along with you this time, so I reckon we'll have to let you get by with it again."

"How are you, Chet?" Slade said as they shook hands. "You're looking well."

"Oh, I was fine till you showed up," sighed Traynor. "Now I'll soon be gaunt as a gutted snowbird from packin' in carcasses."

"Say!" Sheriff Crane exploded in injured tones. "You didn't tell me you knew Traynor!"

"I wished to be sure first that he would acknowledge the acquaintance," Slade said with a smile. "Chet, might as well bring those bodies in and care for the horses. Then we'll explain the whole business."

"Certain," Traynor agreed and led the way to the outside.

"All right, some of you loafers, pack in those carcasses and lay 'em on the floor. Jim will tell you what happened, later; I don't know myself, yet."

The bodies were carried in. Jim was introduced to Shadow and the deputy led the horses to a near-by stable. Sheriff Traynor shooed out the crowd, shut the door, and glanced expectantly at *El Halcón*.

Slade related the various occurrences of the past few days, starting at the beginning, which was the killing of Rafael Vergara. Traynor listened without comment, nodding his big head at times, shaking it at others.

"Juan Covelo," he repeated when Slade paused. "Hart over at Hudspeth County was telling me, a while back, about how the hellion slipped out of your loop after you had busted up his gang. Uh-huh, I've heard of him, a mighty bad sort. And you figure it was Covelo, all right?"

"Little doubt in my mind as to that," Slade replied. Traynor muttered profanity.

"And so the hellions tried to kill you in the Branding Pen

over at Sanderson?" he said, interrogatorily. Slade nodded.

"But I don't think that deal was engineered by Covelo," he explained. "It was too stupid and clumsy. I've a notion some of his underlings got a mite over-eager and tried to move on their own account. Long ago I learned to regard saloon fights with suspicion. Quite often they are used as cover-up; that was how Bowdrie was killed, and Thompson, and Morgan Earp, in a way. It was tried once on Wyatt Earp; didn't work.

"So when that devil started the ruckus by slugging a cow-hand who had his back turned to the carters, I figured something was in the wind. And when the three of them sidled along to the door, I was ready for them."

Traynor shook his head in admiration. "The Mexicans sure have it right when they say the eye of *El Halcón* sees all," he observed. Slade smiled, and did not comment.

"The complicated, carefully thought out scheme to dry-gulch Crane and myself had the Covelo touch," he continued. "And the way it was handled, Covelo stationing himself away from the others, where he could get in the finishing shot if they happened to slip. He made the mistake of shifting his position a little before throwing down on me; I saw a shadow move and had just about lined sights with him when out of the corner of my eye I saw the sidewinder I thought dead raise up with his gun ready for business. Right then I had to forget about Covelo and concentrate on staying alive. Was touch and go; I've a notion if the fellow hadn't been wounded to death, which very likely made him fumble a bit, he would have gotten me before I could throw myself out of line."

"I doubt it," grunted Traynor. "His big mistake was in staying alive that long; would have done better to get it over with and miss being hammered by a few more slugs."

"Rather complicated, but I think I get what you mean," Slade laughed. "He was the sort Covelo manages to get together—his last ambition was to take me with him when he took the big jump."

"And if I don't tie onto something to eat before long, I'll be taking the big jump," Sheriff Crane interrupted. "My stomach's thinkin' my throat's been cut."

"Okay," chuckled Traynor. "We'll amble across the street to a restaurant and grab off a surrounding. Listening to you squawk makes me hungry, too. Jim, the deputy, will be back any minute now and then we'll go."

Jim did arrive a few moments later. "Tell those work

dodgers out there those two hellions tried to drygulch Crane and Slade," the sheriff directed. "That'll hold 'em till I have time to talk to them. Let's go, boys."

Crossing the street, they came to a big and well-lighted restaurant and saloon, somewhat similar to the Branding Pen in Sanderson. The place was crowded and they were the recipient of curious glances as they entered. However, nobody approached them with questions.

"The attempt on Pancho Arista's cart train was in the Covelo manner," Slade added for Traynor's benefit as they sat down to table. "Daring, original, with snake-blooded murder as an adjunct, the true Covelo mode of operation. Oh, he's in a class by himself! Ben Thompson, Doc Skurlock, and Curly Bill Brocius were babes in arms compared to him. As an outlaw leader, Juan Covelo is unique."

"Sure 'pears to be," agreed Traynor. "But he'll get his comeuppance, sooner or later. On that I'll wager a hatful of pesos. Let's eat."

They enjoyed a really excellent dinner with the appreciation of hungry men who know what it is to often find good food scarce. Finally Sheriff Traynor pushed back his empty plate and hauled out his pipe.

"We'll hold an inquest tomorrow," he said. "Reckon you fellers can stand another night in Marathon; she's not a bad town."

"Horses need rest," Slade agreed. "Arista would like for you to send the bodies of his carters to Sanderson for burial."

"Undertaker's got 'em all fixed up decent in good coffins," said Traynor. "The other hellions all go to Boothill in pine boxes. Now what?"

"Now, so far as I'm concerned, a little ear pounding is in order," Slade decided. Crane nodded agreement.

"Good rooms upstairs over this place," supplied Traynor.

"That'll be fine," Slade accepted.

Several prominent citizens came over to the table and received an account of what happened. Crane did the talking and stressed the part Slade played in the affair. The hearers congratulated him on doing an excellent chore.

"Hear tell that young feller is an outlaw himself," one remarked to another after they left the table.

"That so? Well, all I've got to say is that we can use a few more outlaws of his calibre."

"You're darned right!"

Before going to bed, Slade cleaned and oiled his guns, meanwhile cudgeling his brains in an effort to figure what was likely to be Covelo's next move. He did not believe the outlaw leader would attempt another drygulching, having no doubt arrived at the conclusion that trying to drygulch *El Halcón* was a losing game. Whatever it was, it would be something out of the ordinary. What? He hadn't the least idea. To heck with it!

Ten minutes later he was sound asleep.

——— 10

THE INQUEST, held the following afternoon, was a repetition of the one re-
cently held in Sanderson. Slade was again congratulated. The
two sheriffs were advised to rattle their hocks and run down
the rest of the outlaw bunch as quickly as possible, if not
sooner.

Which bit of humor was not appreciated by the peace
officers in question.

Slade and Crane spent another quiet night in Marathon.
Daybreak the following morning found them on their way
back to Sanderson.

"Well, it's nice to have a couple of peaceful days without
anything bustin' loose," commented the sheriff.

"At least nothing we know of," Slade qualified his agreement. He had an uneasy premonition that something had
"busted loose," or would in the near future.

He was not wrong in his surmise.

The trip to Sanderson proved uneventful and they reached
the canyon town shortly after sunset. There everything was
also peaceful and quiet, at least as peaceful and quiet as
Sanderson ever was.

The next day, however, was anything but peaceful. About
mid-morning an angry man stormed into the sheriff's office,
where Slade happened to be at the moment, and shook his
fist under Tom Crane's nose.

"Nigh onto a hundred head of prime stock!" bawled old
John Webb, the Cross W owner. "Nigh onto a hundred head
gone to blazes! What are you going to do about it? Where
you been? Here's a message the telegraph operator asked me
to give you. Said he couldn't deliver it yesterday."

"What, another one!" roared the sheriff. "What the—"

"Hold it," Slade interrupted. "Sheriff Traynor said he sent
you a wire right after he reached town. Of course we were
on the road then." He turned to the wrathful rancher.

"Mr. Webb," he said quietly, "do you know what route your cows followed when they were widelooped?"

"Musta gone through that blankety-blank rackety canyon." growled Webb. "No other way they could do. We trailed 'em almost to the canyon, but there's a rocky stretch nearly a mile wide just north of that blasted hole and we lost the track there. Musta gone through the canyon, though, with a straight shoot to the river."

"Any idea when they were run off?" Slade asked.

"Uh-huh, a pretty good notion," replied Webb. "It rained along toward morning and the tracks showed they were run off after the rain."

"Which, according to your reckoning, would mean a daylight run to the river," Slade observed thoughtfully. "A rather unusual procedure, risking being spotted as they most certainly would have."

"Spotted or not spotted, that's what they did," said Webb. "What are you going to do about it, Crane?"

"I'll do all I can, John; try and trail them," the sheriff replied wearily.

"Heck of a lot of good that'll do," snorted Webb. "I'm going to get a drink."

He stormed out, banging the door behind him. Crane turned to Slade.

"Well, what do you think?" he asked.

"I think," Slade answered, "that those cows did not go through Echo Canyon."

"There's no other way through the hills," Crane protested.

"None that is generally known," Slade said. "But there might be a way that once was known but has been forgotten. The Texas hills are full of old tracks, many of them made by the Indians. Several times in the course of my experience, I have hit on trails where everybody said none existed. Once or twice the place where they reached the level ground was covered by brush. The day of the hunter and trapper is past, and there is nothing in those hills to attract the prospector. And, as you well know, the cowhand seldom leaves the level range which is his habitat. Only by force of circumstances does he venture into the hills. There could be a way through which would provide a direct route to the Rio Grande. If so, and the rustlers know of it, my opinion is that they'd keep the stolen cows holed up in the hills till night-fall before heading them for the river, where quite likely a smuggling boat is waiting to receive them; they'd hardly try to swim that heavily fleshed stock across with the river high as it is now."

"Just what are you getting at, Walt? Just what's on your mind?" Crane asked.

"Tom," the Ranger replied, "I'm going to play another hunch. Get a posse together. You have three deputies, I believe. Right? Okay, the three and a couple of specials you can depend on will be enough. Take your time, there's no rush. And spread the word around that we are heading for Echo Canyon to try and pick up the trail there. That's enough for the present; I'll tell you more later."

"Okay," sighed the sheriff. "You and your hunches! They do always seem to work out, though, and when you can't think of anything I figure it's the smart thing to follow the lead of somebody who can think of something. I'll round up the boys and we'll get goin'."

An hour later, old John Webb watched the posse ride out of town.

"There they go, chasin' their tails!" he snorted to Hardrock Hogan. "Just a waste of time—there won't nothin' come of it."

"I ain't so sure," replied Hardrock. "You'll notice that young feller Slade is with them, and he always 'pears to know what he's about."

"I hope so," growled Webb. "It's sure for certain nobody else hereabouts does."

As the posse rode eastward toward Echo Canyon at a good pace, Slade constantly scanned the back trail. Finally, satisfied they were not being followed, he turned his attention to the trail ahead, studying it carefully, estimating the distance they covered.

After a few more miles they approached a point where a broad stand of tall brush encroached on the track. Slade was confident that from the trail beyond the brush the posse could not be spotted. He concentrated on the bristle of growth as they drew near and arrived at the conclusion that there was nothing worthy of consideration holed up in the chaparral.

Soon they were close to the west straggle. Slade glanced at the westering sun and called a halt.

"Here we turn south," he told Crane. The sheriff shot him a puzzled glance.

"Why?" he asked. "We're still quite a ways from the canyon."

"Which is where we want to be," the Ranger replied.

"Here we turn south and continue until we reach the river. Then we'll turn east again for a few miles, find a suitable spot and await developments. As I recall, not far ahead the river runs straight for quite a distance. The sky is clear and there'll be a bright moon tonight. We will be able to see anything approaching on the water for miles. I feel confident that with a little good luck we'll be able to recover Webb's cows for him and at the same time quite probably rid the section of at least some of the wideloopers, maybe even the big he-wolf of the pack."

"But," protested one of the deputies, "them cows must have crossed the river long ago."

"They did not," Slade stated flatly. "Right now they're holed up somewhere waiting for night. As I mentioned to you, Tom, those cows are heavily fleshed and awkward, and right now the river is high. An attempt to swim them across would very likely result in the loss of about half of them. Also, a buyer would be chary of receiving so large a stolen herd hereabouts. It would mean a long drive to *his* market, the chances are, with the danger of being spotted by the *rurales*, the Mexican Mounted Police, or somebody. So I am of the opinion that swimming them across here won't be risked."

"Then what in blazes will they do with the critters?" the deputy demanded.

"Just this," Slade replied. "Sometime after dark, around toward midnight, I'd say, a steamer—lots of them deal in all sorts of smuggling—will nose in to the bank somewhere along here, let down a section of her side plates to form a loading plank and the rustlers will drive the herd aboard. Off will go the ship downstream to where a buyer is waiting."

"I never heard of such a thing," sputtered the doubting deputy.

"The procedure is not new," Slade answered. "I've encountered it a couple of times. Was used with sheep down around Port Isabel and over at Matagorda Bay. I doubt if it has been used in this section. The weighty improved stock is fairly new here, and the old longhorns would swim the river without difficulty and be all set for a fast drive to market. Things are different now. Cattle stealing is getting to be big business and methods are changing in accordance. I could be wrong, but I'm pretty sure I'm not. Any more questions?"

"There ain't," Sheriff Crane cut in with decision. "What you say to do is what we're going to do; never known you to be wrong yet and I don't figure you'll start now. Just how are you going to work it, Walt?"

"As I said before," the Ranger explained, "we'll jog along till we sight the river—no hurry—then we'll follow the course of the stream until we come to that long straight stretch, locate a suitable spot and hole up and wait. As I figure it, we have everything to gain and nothing to lose except a little sleep."

There was a general nodding of agreement. Even the doubting deputy remarked, "Makes sense to me."

"Let's go," Slade said.

At a moderate pace they continued until they could see the tawny flood of the Rio Grande, streaked with scarlet and rose by the setting sun. Slade still held the present course. Finally, a half mile or so from the river's edge he changed direction and they rode steadily eastward. As the blue dusk closed down, they sighted the straight stretch. And here a scattering of growth followed the course of the stream, thickening now and then to clumps of dense thicket.

At a point where they could see the river for more than a mile in either direction, and also see across the rangeland to the north for a considerable distance, Slade called a halt.

"This is made to order for us," he exulted. "Couldn't be better. Now we can take it easy until something breaks, which I figure won't be for quite a while yet. The chances are the ship will show first, which will be in our favor; we can edge along in the brush until we're all set to cover it and the herd, too. Sure you can smoke. And flip out the bits and let the cayuses graze. As I said, we have plenty of time to wait.

"But," he added impressively, "if it comes to a shooting, and I'm pretty sure it will, make every shot count and don't take chances. Unless I'm making a big mistake, and I don't think I am, we'll be up against as vicious a bunch as Texas ever spawned, vicious and resourceful, with a man at the head of it who has plenty under his hat. Okay, unfork and make yourselves comfortable."

The men proceeded to do so. Physically there was little to complain of. The weather was fine, the grass soft, with plenty of convenient tree trunks for back rests. Old campaigners, the majority of them, they had packed along sandwiches and canteens of coffee that were still warm.

Mentally, however, the going wasn't so easy. The prospect of a desperate fight in the offing tensed nerves a bit, and the tedious wait did not help.

Slade alone appeared unaffected. In fact, he was really enjoying himself; for the time being, at least, the experience savored of a picnic. And his philosophy of "if your number isn't up, nobody can put it up" permitted him to view the coming brush with the outlaws with equanimity.

Sheriff Crane, sensing the placidity of his mind, regarded him with envy.

"Don't nothing ever bother you?" he demanded querulously.

"If it hasn't happened, there's no sense in bothering about it, because maybe it won't. And if it has already happened, bothering about it is just a waste of time and cannot alter the fact," Slade returned.

The sheriff shook his grizzled head, snorted, and puffed hard on his pipe.

The slow hours snailed past. The river was a silver ribbon of mystery dimpled with stars. The rangeland shimmered in the wan light, a ghostly playground for elves and sprites, or so Slade's vivid imagination peopled it. Midnight, the witching hour, was edging down the stream of time and drawing close, close.

11

Suddenly Slade's unusually keen ears caught a sound, a rhythmic sighing, little louder than the faint susurrus of the incoming tide. Swiftly it loudened, became a murmur, a mutter, a monotonous chugging. Slade stood up and gazed toward the distant bend downstream.

Something appeared at the bend, inchoate, vague, a monster of the water, breasting the flood of the Rio Grande, growling and grumbling to itself.

Quickly, however, it assumed form and shape, resolved to a good-sized steamer moving steadily upstream, showing no running lights, the menacing growl and grumble the puffing of her stack.

"Yes, she's showing first, as I figured," Slade said. "Tether the horses back in the brush, and hope they'll keep quiet. We'll wait till she moves in to shore, quite likely in line with that open space in the growth a couple of hundred yards downstream, then we'll ease up as close as we dare."

Slade's surmise was correct. The steamer did nose in to the shore in line with the wide opening in the brush, turning broadside to the bank, her bow upstream. The water was deep and she was able to hold against the bank. Her anchor went down with a splash. Then there was a rattle and clang, a creaking of chains and the whine of a hoisting engine. A ten-foot section of the ship's side was slowly lowered to the bank, providing an adequate loading plank for the expected cattle. Lights flared dimly on the deck, outlining shadowy figures moving about.

"Going to try and drop a loop on the blasted ship, too?" the sheriff whispered to Slade.

"If we can, but the bunch on shore will be our main objective," Slade breathed reply. "All right, ease along through the brush, and for Pete's sake be quiet or the game will be up."

Slowly, carefully, the posse glided through the growth in the wake of the silently treading Ranger. As they crept along, Slade debated the idea of trying to capture the steamer first, but decided against it. To do so would most likely mean a fight with the ship's crew, and the sound of gunfire would carry a great distance in the silent night and perhaps warn the wideloopers and provide them with an opportunity to escape. And it was the rustling band that was his prime quarry. Especially the elusive head of that band. With luck, tonight might prove to be the end of Juan Covelo.

Where the growth began to thin, Slade paused, the others fanning out behind him so as to cover both the loading plank and the approach to it.

From the ship's deck came the sound of rough voices and an occasional laugh. Evidently the steamer's crew had heard nothing to alarm them.

Again the tedious wait, this time without the solace of pipe or cigarette, standing in strained positions, almost afraid to breathe. But there was no help for it. And as the slow minutes dragged past, *El Halcón* began to experience a certain uneasiness. Did the dawn break before the rustlers put in an appearance, the steamer's occupants would most certainly spot the posse and his carefully worked-out plan come to naught.

It was bad enough in the white flood of the moonlight; the growth was scanty and sharp eyes on the deck might at any moment note movement amid the shadows as somebody was forced to shift position. The tension was mounting to the breaking point. Also, while the horses had so far kept quiet there was no guarantee that they would continue to do so indefinitely; let one of the broncs take a notion to sing a song to the morning star and discovery would be almost inevitable.

So it was with a feeling of intense relief that he sensed movement far to the north. Shadowy movement, like to the forward flow of a low-lying cloud, drifting steadily southward at a good pace.

"Get set! Here they come," he whispered to the sheriff, who passed the word down the line.

"They—" he began to reply, "Holy Pete!"

A chorus of excited voices sounded. A searchlight shot a dazzling beam along the open space. From the greater elevation of the deck, the steamer's captain had also sighted the approaching herd and was signaling, "All's well!" with the light.

"Down, crouch down!" Slade hissed. "If they don't spot

us from the ship it'll be all to the good. The light will be in the rustlers' eyes, with us in the shadow. Stay down!"

Breathlessly the posse watched the advancing herd. Aboard the steamer all eyes were also on the coming cows and the tense watchers huddled in the sparse growth were not discovered.

Now the low rumble of hoofs and the thin bleating of the tired and disgusted cattle could be heard. The posse tensed for action.

"Most of the bunch will ride ahead to hold the cows in line for the loading, leaving only a man or two behind to keep the herd moving; I've seen it done before," Slade whispered. "Wait till they're bunched at the water's edge. You do the talking, Tom. We're law enforcement officers and must give them a chance to surrender. I don't think they'll take it, so shoot at the first move. Steady! Here they come."

Into the beginning of the open space streamed the herd. Horsemen came racing along the line of march, all except two who remained behind, riding drag. The first two horsemen reached the water's edge, one on either side of the loading plank. They pulled to a halt facing the column of cows. The others surged forward to join them. The first of the cattle had not yet reached the water's edge.

"Blazes!" muttered Crane. "More than a dozen of the hellions."

"Now!" Slade said. The sheriff's voice rang out, "Elevate, in the name of the law!"

There was a chorus of startled exclamations. The horsemen whirled toward the sound. Another voice pealed through the uproar, "Let them have it!"

Slade shot with both hands. The others fired as fast as they could pull trigger. The outlaws, taken utterly by surprise, unprepared, nevertheless fought back with vicious courage. Back and forth darted the lances of reddish flame. The banging of the guns, the bawling of the terrified cattle, the howls of consternation from the steamer's deck, yells of pain, curses of rage, and the screaming of the frantic horses rose in a hideous turmoil to the shuddering stars.

A yelp of pain sounded behind Slade, and another. Somebody had stopped one. He saw three of the outlaws fall from the saddle, a fourth, a fifth. Penned in by the milling cattle, almost against the gangplank, was the lance-straight figure of a horseman. The moonlight glinted on his yellow hair. Slade fired point-blank, but the other ducked sideways and his answering shot grazed the top of the Ranger's shoulder, throwing him momentarily off balance.

The steamer's stack boomed, pouring forth clouds of black smoke and clots of fire. The paddles beat the water. The hoisting engine chattered frantically. The gangplank slowly rose. The outlaws who remained alive were in full flight, but their leader, Juan Covelo, was still hemmed in by the surging cattle.

Even as Slade regained his balance and lined sights, Covelo whirled his horse and sent it charging toward the rising gangplank. He bellowed a command, the horse screamed protest but took the jump, soaring over the edge of the rising steel, landed on its inward slanting surface and skated forward into the hold. Slade heard his bullet clang on metal as the steel plates slammed shut. Now the demoralized cows had the water's edge blocked. The steamer, her stack roaring, her paddles thrashing the water to foam, plowed away from the bank and toward the middle of the stream. Seething with helpless anger, Slade watched her go.

In the northern distance, a half dozen horsemen were racing their mounts, ineffectual bullets from the posse's guns speeding them on their way. And far, far ahead of them were the two drag riders, who had taken no part in the ruckus but had gotten the heck away from there while the going was good.

But scattered along the water's edge were five motionless forms, some torn and trampled by the maddened cattle, that would never ride again.

"We didn't do so bad," shouted the sheriff. "Got all the cows back and did for five of the hellions. Was that Covelo who went aboard the last minute? Blazes, the chance he took!"

"Yes, that was Covelo," Slade replied. "I saw his yellow hair, and nobody else would have taken such a chance, jumping his horse onto that rising steel platform. If it had caught him as it slammed shut it would have smashed him to a pulp. Yes, it was Covelo. He never misses a bet. I was sure I had him, for he was hemmed in on all sides by the cows. Looked like the only way he could go was into the river, but he saw opportunity and, as usual, took advantage of it with hair-trigger speed and sureness. He outsmarted me again, that's all."

"I figure you did a mite of outsmartin', yourself," grunted Crane. "And I guess everybody else will think so, too."

"Anybody badly hurt?" Slade asked, changing the subject. "I thought I heard somebody yelp."

"One of the specials has got a smashed shoulder, not too good, I'm afraid," replied Crane. "The other caught one in the arm, not bad, I reckon."

Slade stepped to the edge of the brush and whistled a long, loud note. A moment or two later there was a thudding of hoofs and Shadow surged up to him, snorting inquiringly. Slade quickly procured his medicants from the saddle pouches and turned to the wounded.

One of the specials was leaning against a tree, gripping his shoulder with crimsoned fingers and looking rather sick. The other cherished a bullet-punctured arm and was swearing so profusely that Slade concluded he wasn't much hurt.

Without delay he went to work on the injured shoulder, deftly padding and bandaging the member after smearing the wound with antiseptic salve.

"High up, and the slug went straight through without breaking any bones," he told the special. "You'll be okay in a week or two. Sit down, with your back against the tree, and take it easy for a spell. How do you feel now?"

"A devil of a sight better," answered the special, drawing hard on the cigarette Slade rolled for him. "You sure did a prime chore on me. Never heard of a perfessional sawbones who could do a better. Much obliged, feller, a lot."

A pad and a bandage took care of the other special's arm. Sheriff Crane watched the operation, nodding with satisfaction.

"That searchlight sure did us a good turn, as you figured it would," he observed. "Reckon the devils couldn't really see us at all; acted like they were shootin' blind."

"It helped, all right," Slade agreed. "Yes, things didn't work out too bad, even if Covelo did manage to slide out of the loop. Let's have a look at what we downed."

The deputies had kindled a fire to aid the moon and by its light were examining the bodies.

"See they didn't take the trouble to wear their masks this time," observed Crane. "Reckon they felt plumb safe. Which goes to show your *amigo*, Covelo, ain't as smart as he's chalked up to be. He might have known that *El Halcón* would have a trap set for him somewhere."

"The chances are *El Halcón* wouldn't have thought of it if he hadn't previously had experience with similar procedures," Slade deprecated the feat. "As I mentioned to you, running off stolen stock by boat is new to this section, but not farther down the river and along the bays. Anybody recall seeing them before?"

The deputies were of the opinion they had noticed two of the outlaws in town but were noncommittal as to the other three.

"Wonder if any of this bunch rode for John Webb," the sheriff muttered to Slade, with a meaningful glance.

"I wouldn't discuss it, if I were you, unless it turns out to be the case," Slade remonstrated. "Too much loose talk going around as it is."

"Guess you're right," Crane agreed. "Let's see if there's anything worth while in their pockets."

The pockets revealed nothing noteworthy aside from quite a bit of money, that the sheriff confiscated.

"How about some coffee, Slade?" asked one of the deputies. "We still got three canteens left."

Slade's answer was to haul out his little flat bucket and rake together a bed of coals.

"Better when it's hot," he said.

"You're right," chuckled the deputy and filled the bucket to the brim.

The tired cattle had quieted down and were grazing. Slade glanced at the clock in the sky.

"We'll let them rest till daybreak," he decided. "They need it. A little longer spell of taking it easy will be good for the specials, too."

The wounded men were plied with hot coffee and cigarettes and declared they were fit for anything. Both were husky young fellows and Slade did not think the ride to town would do them any harm.

The horses ridden by the dead outlaws had bolted into the brush but reappeared after a while and were captured without difficulty. The bits were flipped out and they were allowed to graze with the others. The posse lounged about the fire, joking and chatting. Everybody, even the wounded men, were in excellent spirits. Slade had recovered from the moment of depression due to Covelo's escape and agreed with the sheriff that they hadn't done so badly.

The moon sank behind the western crags, the stars brightened, then paled as the east flushed rose and gold. Huge vaporous shapes moved over the surface of the river like ghosts of long-forgotten dawns, mists rising from their watery beds to greet the sun.

The posse yawned and stretched. The bodies were roped to

the backs of the outlaws' horses, the cattle rounded up, and the long drive to Sanderson began.

"We'll take the critters right to town with us and corral them," the sheriff decided. "No sense in going on north to Webb's place. Let the old coot come in for them. Figure we'd oughta show 'em off to folks, anyhow."

Nobody objected and the victorious cavalcade moved on, arriving at Sanderson less than an hour before sunset.

The thoroughly worn-out and just as thoroughly disgusted cows were corralled. Doc Cooper was summoned to examine the wounded specials.

"What's the sense in botherin' me?" he grumbled. "Slade looked after 'em, didn't he? Okay, I'll change the bandages and then they can go to bed or get drunk, whichever they are of a mind to."

After the chore was finished, the man with the injured shoulder decided on bed. The other headed for the Branding Pen, doubtless to obey the doctor's orders in his own fashion.

"Inquest at two," said Doc as he packed his bag and departed.

There was excitement a-plenty in Sanderson. Soon the sheriff's office was crowded with folks eager to hear the details of the routing of the wideloopers and the recovery of the stolen cattle. Sheriff Crane and the deputies obliged, and the story lost nothing in the telling. Prominent citizens, including the mayor, shook hands with Slade and spoke words of praise.

"Guess John Webb will sorta tighten the latigo on his jaw after this," chuckled Hardrock Hogan, who had dropped in for a look-see. "He was sure his cows were gone and figured you fellers were just wastin' your time. I told him Slade didn't waste his time and that I was willing to bet he'd get his cows back. He said I was loco and swallerforked out, snortin' like a bull with its tail caught in a barbed wire fence. I've a notion he'll sing another tune tomorrow. One of his hands was in town and headed for the spread to tell him what happened."

"Contrary old shorthorn!" growled the sheriff. "All right, everybody, outside! I crave a surroundin' and some shut-eye. Come back tomorrow."

Before going to bed, Slade, as usual, cleaned and oiled his guns. After a fashion of men who ride much alone, he had a habit of talking to the big sixes when Shadow was not around to commune with.

"Well, Covelo made it in the clear, like he always seems to," he told the Colts. "I've a notion he'll travel down the river for quite some distance, via the boat, before ordering the skipper to put him ashore. In fact, I'm of the opinion that *amigo* Covelo is going to be conspicuous by his absence for the next few days.

"But he'll be back, no doubt as to that. The majority of his hellions also escaped and will be holed up somewhere waiting for him to rejoin them. We haven't seen the last of Juan Covelo, not by a long shot.

"What I've got to do is learn how they run the cows through those hills. Learn that and there's a chance I may be able to drop a loop on the sidewinder. By way of some old forgotten Indian track, I imagine. With its entrance to the rangeland hidden by growth. Well, I've experienced such things before and know what to look for. So we'll wait and see. Didn't do too bad last night, everything taken into account."

He holstered the guns and lay down with a tranquil mind.

——— 12

OLD JOHN Webb showed up around noon the next day, while Slade was eating his breakfast in the Branding Pen. He came over to the table and flopped into a vacant chair.

"Guess I'm here to eat a little crow," he rumbled, sticking out a huge and hairy paw for Slade to shake. "Hardrock Hogan was right and I was wrong. Much obliged, son, and I won't forget it. Anytime I can do you a favor, don't hesitate to ask." He speculated the Ranger a moment, then shook his head.

"Nope, no use to try to make you a little present, sort of a reward for the recovery of stolen property. You ain't the sort to take pay."

"Thank you, Mr. Webb," Slade smiled, taking the compliment as it was meant. Old John snorted, and looked embarrassed.

"But don't forget about the favor part," he reminded. "Reckon I'm on solid ground there."

"You are," Slade assured him. "I consider it an honor to be able to ask." Webb snorted even louder, and looked even more embarrassed, and quickly changed the subject.

"Reckon I know how Arista felt when you saved his carting train," he observed. "I—hey! Here he comes now."

Walt Slade had an inspiration. He caught the carter's eye and beckoned. Arista approached the table, rather hesitantly. Slade bit back a grin as the two elderly gentlemen regarded each other somewhat askance, much in the manner of strange dogs that unexpectedly meet on a narrow path.

"Sit down, Pancho," he said, "I have something to say to both of you." Arista sat down. He and Webb both looked expectant.

"It's no secret," Slade continued, "that you are both in the carting business. It's a good business and could be made better by proper and energetic handling. But it won't be made better by ruthless competition which, if you'll be truthful, I think you both will admit. You have both done me the honor to request that if ever I desired a favor not to hesitate to ask. Well, right now I'm asking a favor of both of you."

Both hearers looked bewildered and a trifle startled. Webb broke the silence.

"What is it?" he asked.

Slade let his steady gaze rest on first one face, then the other.

"Just this," he replied, choosing his words carefully. "That you stop snapping at one another, bury the hatchet, and get together. Combine your two trains and go after new business—there are plenty of sources that have not yet been tapped. By doing so, you will be doing me a favor, yourselves a favor, and doing the community in general a favor. By the attitude you have previously adopted, I hold it more good luck than anything else that you haven't succeeded in getting yourselves into big trouble."

Pancho Arista, doubtless remembering how near he came to shooting one of Webb's cowhands, nodded emphatic agreement.

"Well, what do you say?" Slade asked.

Arista, with Latin impulsiveness, was the first to answer.

"Why," he said, "I can't see that I have any objection to what you propose. How about you, Mr. Webb?"

"Name's John to my friends," growled Webb. "Here's my hand on it—Pancho. I figure we'll pull in double harness okay."

"I'm sure we will—John," said Arista as they solemnly shook.

Old John let out a bellow, "Hardrock! Get us pencils and some paper, will you? I'll make out a list of my equipment, so we can get started on a business-like basis," he said. He whirled on El Halcón.

"Slade," he demanded querulously, "how the devil do you always manage to make everybody do whatever you want them to do?"

"Perhaps by showing them what they've really been wanting to do all along," the Ranger smiled.

"That may be the answer," Arista remarked thoughtfully. "But not many have the divine gift that enables them to point the way to others, and make them see it. Now, John—"

Soon the former antagonists had their heads together over sheets of paper covered with figures and notations. Slade

chuckled under his breath and resumed his interrupted breakfast.

A few minutes later, Sheriff Crane entered the room. He
stopped stock still, stared unbelievingly at the absorbed pair
at the table, shifted his gaze to Slade, threw out his hands in
a despairing gesture, and plunged to the bar.

"What sort of stuff do you sell here, anyway?" he demanded of Hardrock Hogan. "I've only had two snorts so
far today and already I'm seein' things what ain't!"

"Two snorts of the likker *I* sell, and a Gila monster smiles
at a horned toad," Hardrock returned composedly, filling a
glass to the brim.

The following afternoon Walt Slade rode east at a fast
pace. And as he rode, he hummed gaily in his deep, musical
voice. He was composing a song, a song that had come to
him as his gaze rested on the flower-carpeted prairie beautiful under the sun,

"I'll get it before the day is out," he assured Shadow, who
snorted disapproval.

"Better pay attention to what's going on around you instead of making that racket," the snort seemed to say.

"Oh, I figure things will be sorta peaceful for a day or two,"
Slade replied. "Will take *amigo* Covelo a little while to get
reorganized and I imagine his bunch is holed up and keeping
out of sight until he shows up and starts them on the rampage
again. Nothing's going to happen today."

"That's what you think," the answering snort said very
plainly. "Just wait, my friend, just wait!"

Shadow was to prove himself no mean prophet.

Slade's first objective was Echo Canyon. He was very curious as to what was responsible for the most unusual echo
and intended, if possible, to find out.

Curiosity, incidentally, has never been given its proper
importance by philosophers. Besides being fatal to a certain
domestic animal, as an instigating force it has brought joy
and sorrow into the lives of men and women and made and
marred careers. And curiosity had laid hold of a certain
member of old John Webb's household who had been hearing a great deal about one Walt Slade, of late, and had developed an urge to gratify that curiosity.

The results of this would create interesting complications.

When he reached the south mouth of the canyon, Slade
slowed Shadow's pace to a walk and as he rode up the gorge
he studied the walls intently.

Shortly before the death of his father, which occurred after
financial reverses resulted in the loss of the elder Slade's
ranch, young Walt had graduated from a famous college of
engineering. His intention had been to take a postgraduate
course to round out his education and better fit him for the
profession he had determined to make his life's work.

This at the time became impossible, so he lent an attentive
ear when Captain Jim McNelty, his father's friend, and
with whom he had worked some during summer vacations,
suggested that he join the Rangers for a while and devote his
spare time to private study.

Slade signed up with Captain Jim, and found the work
highly interesting and satisfactory. Long since he had gotten
more from private study than he could have hoped for from
any postgrad studies and was eminently fitted to enter the
profession of engineering. His exhaustive knowledge of the
subject, incidentally, had more than once proven valuable
in his Ranger work.

But meanwhile, Ranger work had gotten a strong hold on
him, providing as it did so many opportunities for helping de-
serving people and making the wonderful land he loved a
better place in which to live. So he was loath to sever connections with the illustrious body of law enforcement officers.
He was young and there was plenty of time to be an engineer;
he'd stick with the Rangers a while longer. This decision
caused stern old Captain Jim to chuckle under his mustache.

So as he rode slowly up the canyon, Slade regarded the
peculiar formation with the eyes of an engineer and a geolo-
gist.

For some distance the gorge was deathly still, the silence
broken only by the click of Shadow's irons on the stony
floor. Then a faint sighing became apparent. It loudened to a
murmur, a mutter, a growling rumble. Another moment and
the uncanny echoes were going full blast, filling the canyon
with their tumult, vibrating the rock walls. Slade halted
Shadow and sat staring at the west wall.

The silence swooped down, save for the sibilant murmur
that was Shadow's breathing and the bell clang that echoed
the jingle of a bit iron. Shadow snorted disgustedly and got a
booming reply. But Slade was quick to note that the horse
showed no signs of perturbation, just irritation at the hulla-
baloo.

He studied the west wall, his glance running up and down,
back and forth. It was cracked and fissured, and many of the
fissures were quite wide and long, with nothing but darkness

behind them. And that was all; so far as he could see there was nothing remarkable about the configuration of the cliffs, nothing out of the ordinary; he had seen many similar ones. The whole outlandish business just didn't seem to make sense. He shook his head and rode on to the accompaniment of demoniac bursts of sound. And when he reached the north mouth of the guard, the racket ceased as if it had been cut off by a knife.

"Well, we haven't learned anything so far," he remarked to the horse. "Maybe we can do better up on top of the east cliffs. The other time we were up there we had other things to think about. Just possible that we overlooked something. Okay, up you go, it isn't a hard pull and the growth isn't too bad. Just a minute, though."

Before breasting the slope he cast an all-embracing glance at his surroundings. Nowhere did anything move. The hills and the rangeland appeared devoid of life.

Which was what he expected. He was confident that there would be no activity by Covelo and his bunch for a few days.

But just the same, as he ascended the long slope sharp eyes watched his every move.

In due time he reached the crest without incident. Close to the edge of the cliff he dismounted, rolled a cigarette, and stood gazing into the shadowy depths, once again studying the west wall, and learning nothing.

And all the time, the eyes of an unseen watcher were studying *him*.

For quite a while he stood staring absently into the canyon, humming under his breath the tune of the song he had been composing. Abruptly he turned to Shadow, his eyes twinkling.

"Got it, horse," he announced. "Got a title for it, also— 'To the Texas Bluebells.' How's that? Want to hear it? Okay, here we go."

Shadow snorted resignedly, but pricked his ears forward in anticipation. He loved music, as his master well knew. So Slade flung back his black head and sang. Sang of how the flowers awoke to the first sweet promise of spring, creeping timidly forth from winter's dark caverns into the glorious sunshine that now was so warm and gentle, unveiling their beauties to the golden Lord of Day, filling the air with their fragrance, holding up their dew-filled cups in homage.

Sang of how the Queen of the Elves touched the Texas bluebells with her magic wand and gave unto them a voice the other flowers could hear, and heed.

And as the great golden baritone-bass pealed and thundered to the sky, the unseen watcher stood entranced—and amazed. Could this be the cold killer whose name was on every tongue? The grim fighting man who outfaced desperate odds, himself the very stroke of the grim reaper's scythe—this tall, laughing-eyed singer of dreams?

The song ended in a burst of exquisite melody.

> And call the flowers to vespers
> When the summer day is done.
> And that is why the bluebells
> Chime sweetly to the sun

His eyes still laughing, Slade spoke to his equine audience. "Well, horse, how do you like it? Okay? *Gracias!*"

The hidden watcher glided forward another step on silent feet—silent until he trod on a dry branch hidden under the leaves, that broke with a sharp snap.

The results were bewildering, and alarming. All the laughter gone from his eyes, Slade hurled himself sideways in a ripple of motion, a long gun just "happening" in his hand, ready for business. But for once, *El Halcón* was "caught settin'!"

13

She stepped composedly from the growth, apparently oblivious to the black muzzle yawning in her direction, and looked him up and down. She wasn't very big, but even well-worn Levi's and soft blue shirt, open at the throat, declared loudly—nothing to be desired! Her eyes *were* big, and dark blue. She had dark, curly hair, creamily-tanned cheeks, very red lips, and a straight little nose, the bridge delicately powdered with a few freckles.

"S-sorry!" stuttered the flabbergasted Ranger, surreptitiously holstering his gun. "I—I mistook you for a—bear."

"Yes, I imagine Mr. Walt Slade is in the habit of making such mistakes," she replied dryly, her voice soft and low.

"You know my name!" he said, once again slightly off balance.

"I would say everybody in three counties knows it," she answered. "It's about all I've been hearing for the past few days. Uncle John and the boys have been praising you to the skies. Of late, they can't seem to think of anything else to discuss."

"Uncle John?" he repeated.

"Yes, John Webb. His sister was my mother; I'm Mary Merril."

"Very euphonious," he said, recovering his customary aplomb. Her eyes widened slightly at his use of the adjective and she glanced at his cowhand garb. However, she did not comment.

"I hope I didn't startle you," he added.

"Not in the least," she answered. "I didn't think even you would shoot a woman."

"Even *me?*"

"I gather you make a specialty of shooting people. Or so everybody says. I'll admit frankly I became quite curious about you and hoped to get a look at such a terrible person, but I hardly expected to under such unusual circumstances."

Slade laughed. "Well, after all it would appear there is recompense for being notorious," he said. "But what I'd like to know is how did you manage to ride up here without me seeing you."

"I didn't," she explained. "I was here when you arrived. I often ride up here. I like to listen to the echoes. When there is no other sound and the wind blows through the canyon, they are purest music."

Which of course explained the recent usage of the track by which he had reached the crest on the occasion of his former visit, and that had puzzled him at the time.

"Ordinarily they are anything but musical," he replied, apropos of the echoes. "Almost as bad as the racket I kicked up a while ago."

"Don't fish for compliments, Mr. Slade," she retorted. "You have a wonderful voice, and you know it. And the song was beautiful; I never heard it before."

Slade smiled and didn't trouble to explain that nobody else had, either.

"How did you come to know me when you saw me?" he asked.

"From Uncle John's description," she answered. "Really, though, you don't look as terrible as I anticipated."

"Looks are ofttimes deceptive," he said. She was gazing at Shadow.

"Also, you have the most beautiful horse I ever saw," she said. "The boys have been raving about him. I would have known you from the horse." She reached a hand.

"Don't touch him!" Slade snapped.

"Horses and I—" she began. The next instant fingers like rods of woven steel clamped her arm and jerked it back as Shadow lunged with bared teeth.

"You little idiot!" he stormed, giving her a shake that clicked her teeth together, for it had been too blasted close for comfort. "Didn't I tell you not to touch him?"

The blue eyes blazed. "Mr. Slade," she said, as stormily as he, "I'm not accustomed to having a man put rough hands on me!"

"Get accustomed to it if you insist on doing fool things," he told her. "Another inch and you'd have lost half your arm. Nobody can touch him without my permission. After this, when I tell you to do something, do it!"

For a moment their glances locked, then abruptly her dark lashes drooped.

"Yes, Mr. Slade," she said, very softly. "Now may I stroke him?"

"It's okay, Shadow," Slade answered obliquely. The black horse's flattened ears pricked forward and he craned his neck toward the girl, thrust his muzzle into her hand and blew softly.

"He understands exactly what you say to him," she marveled.

"Yes," Slade replied, his temper still a bit ruffled because of the narrowness of her escape. "Yes, he does. Better than some people I can mention."

The blue eyes started to blaze again, then abruptly they softened. She spoke, in a low, thrilling whisper, "Listen! The wind!"

Slade heard it, too, a haunting threnody, like horns of elfland softly blowing, rising, falling, dying to a whisper of sound, swelling, murmuring, ceasing but to begin again.

"What can cause it?" breathed the girl. "Those holes in the cliffs?"

Slade shook his head. "The contours of the cliffs do not tend to substantiate such an assumption," he replied.

Again her expressive eyes widened a trifle.

"It is something beyond the surface of the cliffs," he continued. "Back there somewhere is something like to a giant tuning fork that sound waves cause to vibrate. What? I have no idea, at the moment."

His eyes grew thoughtful as he spoke and the concentration furrow deepened between his black brows, a sure sign *El Halcón* was doing some serious thinking.

The weird music of the wind-echoes began again, moaning, sobbing, rising and falling, an eerie fantasia, now lilting, now sinking to a pulse-slowing coronach as the breeze lessened, rising once more to a dulcet rhythm.

"It is lovely, but it makes one sad," the girl murmured.

"Yes, perhaps through a sheer excess of beauty," he replied.

She had instinctively moved closer to him as they listened. He slipped a long arm about her trim waist. She snuggled still a little more closely, looked up into his face. Suddenly a wave of color mantled her cheeks and her white brow. Her lashes dropped but she did not lower her head. He leaned over, and their lips met.

"I think," she said slowly, a little later, "that you are more dangerous than you have been said to be—where a woman is concerned, Mr. Slade."

"And I think," he smiled, "that now we can discard formality. I believe you know my first name."

"Yes—Walt," she said. "And you said mine is—euphonious was the word you employed, I believe."

"It is—Mary."

For several moments they stood silent, while the echoes seemed to sing a more joyful note. She stepped forward a little, gazing into the depths.

"Careful," he warned, tightening his hold on her. "You could slip."

"Might be a good way to solve a problem," she answered with a little sigh.

Slade laughed gaily. Reaching down, he picked her up, cradled her in his arms and moved to the crumbling edge of the cliff.

"A solution for both of us," he said.

Mary smiled and shook her curly head. "I think," she said softly, "that we should be able to discover a more pleasant solution to—problems."

"I think so, too," he agreed cheerfully. He stepped back and dropped her lightly to her feet.

Shadow, who had been watching this bit of byplay with a bored expression, gave a derisive snort, as much as to say, "Here we go again!"

Mary glanced at him and giggled, as if she understood horse language. Perhaps she did.

"Over there," she said, "is a nice comfortable-looking flat rock. Suppose we sit down and—talk."

"Suits me," he answered, suiting the action to the word. "Now what shall we talk about?"

"A man usually talks about himself," she retorted.

"There are exceptions," he countered.

"All right," she said, "then I'll talk about you. It appears you persuaded Uncle John and Mr. Arista to stop fighting and get together."

"I think they'll pull well in double harness," he nodded.

"It was a wonderful thing you did," she declared. "It made me very happy. To me the whole affair didn't make sense. I told Uncle John so the other night, and gave him a good scolding."

"Which doubtless made easier the chore of getting them together," Slade commented.

"Perhaps," she conceded, "but it took you to get them together. How in the world did you do it?"

"I didn't," he denied. "I just suggested it was the sensible thing to do."

"I fear you tend to belittle your persuasive powers," she replied. "Also, I heard how you saved Uncle John's herd, and how you avenged poor Rafael Vergara's murder. And how you saved Pancho Arista's cart train. Oh, I've heard a great deal about you."

"Gossip is fleet of foot," he said.

"I put very little credence in gossip," she returned. "The hard facts concerning you are conclusive enough. Enough to cause *me* to arrive at certain conclusions."

"Yes?"

"Yes. Among others, that you are something quite different from what you allow certain people to believe."

"What do you mean by that?" he asked, a trifle uneasily.

"Oh, just feminine intuition, perhaps, or putting two and two together and making five. Anyhow, even on a deserted cliff top alone with the notorious *El Halcón*, I am not in the least afraid of him."

Slade studied her a moment, then tried a counter-stroke in the dark.

"Nor of yourself?"

"That," she replied, "is a different story." And she didn't smile when she said it.

The sudden renewal of the wind-drifted music of the echoes brought to a close a conversation that, perhaps, had continued long enough, for the time being.

For a while they sat silent, listening. Finally Slade glanced at the low-lying sun, the lower edge of which was already not far from the horizon.

"Don't you think it's about time you were heading for home?" he suggested. "Be dark when you get there as it is, I'm afraid."

"Yes, I suppose I should," she replied. "Uncle John will worry if I'm out too long after dark, and it's seven miles and more to the *casa*."

She glanced at him and smiled, a trifle tremulously.

"Will you ride with me?" she asked. "Uncle John and the boys will be very glad to see you."

"I expect it isn't a bad idea," he agreed. "It will be past dark when you reach home, if it's seven miles to the ranch-house. Where's your horse?"

"Over there to the right, nosing around," she replied. "In a little clearing where there's some grass. I'll get him."

"I'll go with you," he volunteered. "Come along, Shadow."

With the black horse pacing sedately after them, they made their way through the brush to the clearing, where a sturdy little roan stood looking contemplative. Mary flipped the bit into place and started to mount. But before she got her toe in the stirrup, Slade picked her up and tossed her into the saddle.

"You're terribly strong!" she gasped as she fitted her feet to the stirrups.

"The strong can be gentle," he smiled. The answering smile he received was enigmatic.

"Over to the right a little farther is the easiest way down," she said, taking the lead.

The descent was easier than the route by which he had ascended the slope and they soon reached the level ground.

As usual, Slade scanned his surroundings in all directions. There was nobody in sight; the rangeland stretched lonely and deserted.

Mary turned east by slightly north. She gestured to the range of hills to the north.

"The ranchhouse is east of the hills and a little farther north," she said.

Slade nodded and they rode on at a good pace.

They had covered some distance when Slade glanced back the way they had come; his gaze fixed. Just west of the canyon mouth and also riding east by slightly north was a band of horsemen, eight in number.

14

"Now WHERE in blazes did that bunch come from?" Slade wondered aloud. "Certainly they were not anywhere in sight just a few minutes back."

"From the canyon?" Mary guessed. Slade shook his head.

"I don't think so. I'd have surely heard the racket the echoes would have picked up. But where *did* they come from?"

He gazed back at the group, now only about eight hundred yards to the rear. They rode purposefully and he could make out the whitish blur of their faces. His brows drew together.

"Speed up a bit," he told his companion. She shot him a glance but did so without comment. Slade continued to watch the bunch behind. Quickly he realized that they, too, had quickened their pace.

"I don't like the looks of this," he muttered. "Get all you can out of that jughead."

Again she obeyed without question; but it was soon apparent that the roan was no speed horse. The bunch behind was closing the distance. Now the eight hundred yards had shrunk to little more than seven. Another moment and something sang past overhead. Another slug followed the first, a little closer.

"Good heavens!" Mary exclaimed. "I believe they're shooting at us!"

"They are," he replied grimly. "Give him the spurs, hard!"

Bullets continued to whistle past. Slade felt cold all over. And for once in his life, *El Halcón*, the fearless, was thoroughly scared. At that distance they couldn't tell that his companion was a woman. And if they were Covelo and his devils, which Slade firmly believed to be the case, she'd be better off dead than in their hands. He set his teeth as a slug whistled so close he felt the wind of its passing. He glanced despairingly at the laboring roan. The little horse was giving its best, but it wasn't enough. At any moment one of the slugs would find a mark.

One did! The roan gave an almost human scream, staggered, reeled, and fell. Mary kicked her feet free from the stirrups but was thrown heavily. Unable to rise, she writhed on the ground.

Slade jerked Shadow to a rearing halt. He slid his Winchester from the saddle boot and raced back to where the girl lay; now she was on hands and knees and apparently not badly hurt.

"Keep down!" he snapped as he surged past her. "Do as I say!"

Between her and the advancing horsemen, whose yells of triumph he could now hear, he dropped to one knee, threw the Winchester forward.

The muzzle spurted flame and smoke. One of the riders threw up his hands and fell to the ground. The riderless horse swerved sideways, banged into another one. For a moment the pursuers were thrown off balance.

Slade regretfully held the muzzle low. The Winchester spoke again. A horse went down, catapulting its rider over its head. Another fell over it. Now the pursuit was in thorough confusion. Slade fired two more quick shots, saw a man lurch in the saddle. He whirled, scooped up the girl and sped to where Shadow stood.

"Can you stand?" he panted.

"Yes," she answered.

He dropped her to her feet, mounted and reached down and hauled her up in front of him, still clinging to the rifle. His voice rang out, "Trail, Shadow, trail!"

The black horse shot forward, his hoofs drumming the ground. Slade glanced back. The discomfited pursuers had untangled themselves and were speeding in pursuit, shooting and yelling; only six of them now, but still too blasted many. The slugs were coming close again. Shadow was holding his own, so far, but with the double burden, part of it in a very awkward position, he could not draw away from the pursuit.

"Walt!" Mary shrilled. "I believe I know how to throw them off. Turn and ride straight for the hills to the north, toward that canyon mouth a little to the right."

Slade obeyed without question. He didn't see how the situation could get any worse. He doubted if they could pull away from the devils in the canyon, but at least it would be shadowy there, the sun having set; the shooting would not be so good as on the open prairie. With bullets whining around them, they sped for the narrow gorge. They reached it, but meanwhile the pursuers, taking the short leg of the triangle, had lessened the distance. A few more of Shadow's long strides and they were in the canyon and free from the threat of lead for a few minutes.

Mary had twisted around in his arms and was facing to the right, watching the canyon wall that flickered past.

"The next canyon to the right," she cried. "No, not this one, the next one."

They flashed past a gloomy opening and just as the beat of the following horses' irons sounded at the canyon mouth, Slade jerked Shadow sharply to the right and they whisked into another and narrower gorge that ran almost due east.

Now Mary was watching the north wall. A few more minutes and she cried, "To the left at the next opening—just a little ways ahead. Now! Now!"

Again Slade swerved his mount into another and still narrower opening, almost dark. He slowed the blowing horse's pace a little and listened intently.

"I believe that did it," he said. "I can't hear anything."

"Maybe," she agreed, "but turn again at the next opening. Just a few hundred yards ahead. Confound it! It's so dark I can't see!"

"Don't worry, I can," he assured her cheerfully.

He could, and made the final turn successfully. After which he slowed the laboring horse to a walk.

"Well, little lady, I guess you saved our bacon for us," he told the girl. "I was beginning to figure it was curtains."

"Lucky that I've prowled these hills all my life and know every crack and corner of them," she answered. "This canyon leads through the hills and opens onto our south pasture. We've nothing more to worry about. And now that it's all over, I'm scared blue."

"You sure don't act scared," he chuckled. "And you never did, all the while."

"Things were happening too fast for me to find time to get scared," she replied, "but now I am. Please hold me a little closer!"

"I hope you stay scared indefinitely," he said, with another and louder chuckle as he acceded to her request. "This better?"

"Much," she replied. "Now I feel a *lot* better."

Both perfectly satisfied with the status quo, they allowed Shadow to choose his own gait and catch his breath, which last he quickly did. However, he did not quicken his pace. Shadow was a very knowing horse.

"My poor Bunty, my horse," Mary said. "He was dead, was he not?"

"Yes, drilled dead center. Hardly knew what hit him."

"And those were members of the outlaw band you have been fighting with?" she asked.

"They were, no doubt as to that," he replied. "I figured you'd be better dead than captured by them."

She shuddered. "And they were after you, trying to kill you?"

"Well," he smiled, "they sure weren't throwing kisses at me."

She was silent for a moment, then, "You could have easily outdistanced them on Shadow, and escaped."

"Possibly," he conceded.

"But that, of course, never occurred to you."

"Definitely not, circumstances being what they were," was his answer.

"And you risked your life to save mine."

"Well," he said, "I figured that if the big jump was in order, we'd take it together."

"Which perhaps wouldn't have been too bad," she said. "I don't believe I was ever terribly afraid to die, especially in pleasant company."

Slade laughed aloud; she had a delicious sense of humor.

"Okay," he chuckled, "but I think I prefer to have you alive and kicking."

For some reason, best known to herself, the remark caused her to giggle.

A little later, they rode out of the canyon mouth and onto the open rangeland. The night was dark, but overhead the roses of the sky bloomed in all their silver beauty. A whippoorwill called, a coyote yipped cheerfully. And amid the waving grassheads the Texas bluebells blossomed.

"It is good to be alive," she said softly.

"Yes," he agreed. "It is a wonderful land we live in, with so much good to offer to all. It is a blessed privilege vouchsafed to all of us to try and make it better for those who appreciate it. Yes, a privilege we should accept with humble pride."

The girl gazed up at the sternly handsome face outlined

in the starlight; his eyes were gazing into the far distances. She drew a deep breath.

"The understanding heart," she murmured, and was silent.

15

SLADE, TOO, was silent, for he was thinking hard, reviewing what had occurred. After all, he hadn't done so badly, a lot better than the way things looked for a while. He felt fairly convinced he had done away with another member of Covelo's bunch and had wounded a second. And very likely the gentleman who took a header when his horse fell wasn't feeling any too good at the moment.

Of course it was too much to hope that Covelo himself had taken his lethal bullet—that would be completely out of line with the way things usually worked out for Covelo, but at least he must have gotten something of a jolt. With what appeared to be all the advantages on his side, he had bungled the chore. Slade chuckled to himself as he visioned the outlaw leader's discomfiture.

Immediately, however, he was serious, for one question still plagued him—where in the devil did the outlaw bunch come from? The logical answer was that there was a way through the hills known to the outlaws. Well, it was up to him to find it. He had discovered such hidden ways before, where everybody insisted there were none. No reason why he should fail this time. And if he did discover it, there was a good chance to set a trap for the slippery owlhoot that he wouldn't be able to slide out of. How? Slade hadn't the slightest idea, at the moment. First thing was to find the hidden route by which stolen cows were driven south.

The girl seemed to sense his perplexity. Anyhow, she alluded to it obliquely.

"There are many old Indian tracks through the southern hills," she remarked. "I have ridden several that appeared to come from nowhere and go nowhere. Wouldn't you think that by way of one such those men so unexpectedly appeared?"

"Logical to believe so," he replied. "That is unless they were holed up in the brush waiting for us, which certainly doesn't seem reasonable. On the cliff top we couldn't have been seen from the level ground. And despite his undoubted shrewdness, I don't think Juan Covelo is clairvoyant."

Again the big blue eyes widened slightly; this time she spoke what was in her mind. "Your choice of words is unusual for—"

"An outlaw?" he finished smilingly.

"Oh, stop it!" she snapped. "You're no more an outlaw than—than Uncle John. And I have a very good notion what you really are."

"We'll just forget that," he replied.

Her red lips set determinedly.

"All right, you won't tell me, but you will, sooner or later. A woman knows how to make a man talk."

"And when?" he added meaningly.

Even in the starlight her blush was apparent. "Yes, darn it! When!" she retorted. "Look! There's the ranchhouse."

Slade had already noticed the big and sprawling building dimly outlined in the star gleam. A downstairs window was brightly lighted.

"Guess Uncle John is looking for me and wondering what I'm doing out this time of night," Mary said. "I wouldn't be surprised if I'm spanked and put to bed without any supper, and I'm starved."

As they rode up to the veranda, a door opened and John Webb came out. He stared, his head thrust forward.

"What in blazes!" he exploded. "Mary! What happened? Where's your horse?"

"Tell you everything in a minute," she answered as Slade dropped her lightly to the ground. "First I want Shadow taken care of. Next to Walt, he's responsible for me being here and not dead, like my poor horse."

The amazed rancher sputtered profanity, then let out a bellow. A moment later a wrangler came hurrying. He was properly introduced to Shadow and led the big black to a stall. Slade and Mary mounted the steps together. Old John, now speechless with amazement, led the way to the living room, the furnishings of which gave every indication of the wealth of their owner. John Webb, Slade decided, was bountifully endowed with this world's goods.

Webb gestured them to chairs and found his voice. "Now will you please tell me what the blankety-blank is the meaning of all this?"

"Watch your language, dear," Mary reproved. "Yes, I'll tell you."

She proceeded to do so, vividly, stressing the part Slade played. Old John muttered oaths under his breath. When she paused, he turned to Slade.

"Son," he said heavily, "I'm mighty, mighty deep in your debt. She's all I've got left."

"And you won't have me long if I don't get something to eat and soon," the girl declared, jumping to her feet. "Walt must be starved, too. I'll tell the cook to get busy."

She bounced out, flashing a smile at Slade over her shoulder. Old John shook his head.

"I've always been scared something might happen to her, maverickin' around over the country alone like she does. Will take me quite a while to get over this."

"I think she is quite capable of taking care of herself, under ordinary circumstances," Slade assured him. "Circumstances today were a little out of the ordinary."

"Rather," growled Webb. "What in blazes is this section coming to that a woman can't take a ride without having to dodge lead!

"And if she hadn't run into you like she did, she might have run into those sidewinders alone."

Slade nodded without comment; he had already thought of that unpleasant contingency.

"Yes, she was mighty, mighty lucky in meeting up with you," Webb resumed. "I've a notion those devils would have no more mercy for a woman than for a man."

"They wouldn't," Slade agreed.

Old John regarded him fixedly for a moment. "Son," he said, "I don't put no stock in that El Halcón the outlaw sheep dip, but swallerforkin' around like you do, there's always a chance that you'll get into real trouble. Why not settle down? This is a nice section, and I can use you. I'll be needin' a range boss who can really run things, 'fore long; mine is going into business for himself. I'd be mighty, mighty pleased if you'd sign up with me. And," he added shrewdly, "I've a notion Mary would be, too." He paused, then, "And I gotta admit that it gets sorta lonesome in this big old house every now and then, with only Mary around. Yes, I would be mighty glad to have you. And," he said meaningly, "it will all go to her when I pass on; she's the only kin I've got left. And it's a valuable holding. What do you say?"

"I promise you to think on it, very seriously," Slade replied. "And thank you, very much, for the offer and for thinking well of me. I appreciate both."

"Do that," said Webb, "think on it, and I hope you'll take me up on it."

Meanwhile, a conversation was going on in the kitchen between Mary Merril and the Mexican cook.

"*El Halcón!*" he exclaimed. "Now indeed will I prepare the feast fitting to the honored guest."

"You seem to think well of him, Miguel," the girl observed.

"*Señorita,*" replied the cook, "when *El Halcón* sits at our table, it is as if our Lord Himself breaks bread with us."

"Who is he, Miguel, what is he?" she asked.

"He is *El Halcón*, the good, the compassionate, the friend of the lowly. He is a strange man. Where there is trouble, or sorrow, or wrong, *El Halcón* appears. When he departs he leaves behind him happiness and peace. He is hated by those who are evil, loved by those who are good. He is *El Halcón*. Of him I know as much, or as little, as anyone, but it is the great honor to serve him."

"I see," the girl said. "I, too, Miguel, think he is wonderful."

The old cook regarded her in a fatherly way. "*Señorita,*" he said, "you I have known since when you were a tiny *muchacha,* and to you I may speak freely. He is good and he is kind, but he goes where duty calls, and it is a lonely trail, a lonely trail. You cannot cage an eagle, *cara mía.* Caged, it pines and dies.

"But," he added gently, "maybe the touch of a woman's hand can make even a cage a delight."

"I hope you are right, Miguel," she replied, her eyes clouded, her red lips quivering a little.

Abruptly she threw off her somber mood and her lips smiled, her eyes danced.

"Gather ye rosebuds while ye may!" she quoted gaily. "And sometimes a bud blossoms to a beautiful flower that does not wither—for a while."

"That is so," said Miguel and got busy with pots and pans, Mary lending him a hand.

In the living room, Slade remarked to Webb, "I'd like to wash up before I eat; out back?"

"Nope," John replied. "We're modern folks here and we've got a real bathroom. Big spring up the hill, tank on the roof, with a hydraulic ram down below that keeps it fulla water. Come on, I'll show you."

He stumped up the stairs, Slade following.

In the nicely appointed bathroom, Slade enjoyed a good

clean-up. When he descended to the living room, he met Mary on the stairs.

"I'm going to change," she announced. "What Miguel is dishing up calls for something more than overalls and a flannel shirt. Hope you'll be pleased."

"You'd look wonderful in anything, or in—" he began.

She stopped his voice with a rosy fingertip. "Never mind," she said. "Just bend your tall head a little. I want to give you back the one you gave me there on the hilltop."

This time his lips came down on hers, hard, and he crushed her to him. She was trembling a little when he released her, and his own pulses had accelerated quite a bit.

"Whe-e-ew! That will do—for now," she breathed and trotted up the stairs.

She descended as Miguel was calling them to dinner, wearing something which defied masculine powers of description but which Slade thought enhanced her charms. Together they enjoyed the repast Miguel thought commensurate to the occasion. Slade thanked him in fluent Spanish and the old fellow beamed.

"It seems all you have to do to make people happy is speak to them," Mary sighed.

"Are you happy?" he returned laughingly.

"To an extent," she replied.

"Then just speaking is not enough for you?"

Her dark lashes drooped. "No!"

Afterward, they sat in the living room and talked for a while, old John having rambled off to bed. Finally Mary glanced at the clock.

"It's late," she said. "Uncle John sleeps in the back of the house," she added irrelevantly, and giggled as she extinguished the lamp. They groped up the dark stairs together.

16

SLADE WAS awakened the following morning by the hands making ready for breakfast. He dressed, washed, and descended to the living room, where he found Mary and Webb awaiting him. Old John greeted him boisterously, but Mary's eyes were downcast, her cheeks rosy. He cast her a laughing glance, and the roses bloomed still brighter.

At breakfast, Slade met the Cross W hands, including those who had the row with the carters in the Branding Pen, and the young fellow he saved from getting gunned by Pancho Arista. He liked them and concluded that there was no real harm in any of them.

In the living room, after breakfast, Mary asked, "What do you plan to do today, Walt?"

"I wish to have a look at those hills down to the southwest," he replied.

"May I go with you?"

He shook his head.

"No," he answered, "I want you to stay home until things cool down a bit. Now don't argue, do as I tell you."

"Don't I always," she sighed. "I don't think you have any cause for complaint."

"I'm not complaining. I just aim to take care of you," he replied. "You're too precious to lose this early in the game."

"That helps a little," she said. "But you'll be careful, won't you, dear? You might meet those awful men again."

"Nothing to worry about with Shadow packing single," he assured her. "He can show heels to anything in Texas."

"Yes, but it would be just like you to stop and shoot it out with all of them," she remarked morosely.

Slade shook his head. "Nope, odds of six or seven to one are a mite lopsided."

To tell the truth, however, he rather hoped the bunch would try chasing him again. With Shadow's speed, his own extraordinary eyesight, and his high-powered Winchester, the odds wouldn't be as lopsided as appeared on the surface.

He had little hope of that, though; he felt that Covelo and his bunch had had enough of him on the open prairie.

"You'll come back?" she asked as she stood with her cheek against Shadow's neck.

"Of course," he replied. "Tomorrow, if things work out right."

Old John added his own invitation. "And take care of yourself, son, and don't forget what we talked about last night," he said. "I'll be in Sanderson later today, for a conflab with Arista. May see you there."

"Wouldn't be surprised," Slade conceded. "So long."

Leaving the Cross W ranchhouse, Slade rode south by a little west until the southern hills loomed close. Then he rode parallel to them and some little distance out on the prairie, for he knew there was scant chance of spotting a trail near their bases.

So he studied their upper slopes intently, meanwhile not forgetting to continually survey his more immediate surroundings. The old trails, as he was well aware, were beaten hard by myriads of moccasined feet through the course of the centuries, so that they absorbed little rain water. As a result, growth on their surface was scant where it existed at all. Which meant that the course of the trail was marked by an indenture in the brush that could be spotted by keen eyes. More than once, in the past, he had by a similar procedure discovered a trail where none was supposed to exist.

But as he covered mile after mile with no indications of the existence of such a phenomenon, he gradually developed a sense of baffled bewilderment. Nothing could have been more meticulous than his survey of the slopes, and nothing more barren of accomplishment.

Finally he reached the western terminus of the hills, no great distance from Sanderson, still with negative results.

"But, blast it, horse, there must be a way across," he told Shadow. "They didn't fly those cows over, that's sure for certain. And where did that bunch come from yesterday, if not by some obscure track? Well, we'll try again, tomorrow maybe, against the chance we overlooked something."

He turned south and rode steadily until he reached the east-west trail, by way of which he continued to Sanderson and a consultation with Sheriff Crane.

He found that peace officer busy in his office and regaled him with an account of his adventures and misadventures, some of them, at least.

"Looks like they're still after you hot and heavy," he commented when Slade paused.

"Yes, and for a while yesterday it looked like they might put it over," the Ranger returned. "Was touch and go for a while." The sheriff nodded.

"I know Mary Merril," he observed. "A fine gal. Old John dotes on her. She'll inherit the Cross W some day, and it's a darn good holding. And Webb has other resources, too. She'll be a rich woman. You could do a lot worse."

"Who said anything about doing worse, or better," Slade retorted.

Crane chuckled, and practically repeated what John Webb said the night before. "About time you settled down a mite, and there's nothing like a good woman to hold a man steady and keep his cinches from slipping. She's a purty gal, too."

Slade felt it was about time to change the subject and proceeded to do so.

"Anything happen while I was gone?" he asked.

"Nope," Crane replied. "Reckon Covelo is too busy chasin' you to have time for any other hellishness. 'Pears you've got him on the run, before or after you."

"I'm beginning to wonder which is which," Slade said with irritation.

"Anyhow, it 'pears you've busted up a cart war," observed Crane. "You could have knocked me over with a feather when I saw Webb and Arista sitting at that table with their heads together."

"Webb said he expected to be here later in the day," Slade remarked. "He and Arista have some matters to discuss."

"Quite a relief to have them discussing 'em with pencils instead of six-shooters," grunted the sheriff. "Yep, you did a mighty good chore there."

"But I haven't done the one I was sent here to do," Slade pointed out. "Covelo and his hellions are still mavericking around."

"Quite a few of them ain't mavertickin' any more, at least not topside the ground," Crane observed dryly. "I ain't worried; just a matter of time."

"Hope you're right," Slade said. "Well, how about ambling over to the Branding Pen for a cup of coffee and a snack? Been quite a while since breakfast, and not finding the things I'm looking for makes me hungry."

"Guess we could do worse," the sheriff agreed. "Let's go."

In the Branding Pen they found an isolated table where they could talk, sat down and gave their orders. Crane chattered away on various subjects, but Slade was mostly silent, occupied with his own thoughts.

These dealt chiefly with the question how the blankety-blank blue blazes the wideloopers ran those cows across the Tonto Hills with their precipitous, almost straight-up-and-down slopes, rock-strewn and thickly grown with a tangle of throny brush. There must be some way to overcome that seemingly insurmountable barrier, for the fact remained that the cows did get across.

And in the back of his mind was a vague feeling, little more than a formless hunch, that somehow Echo Canyon had something to do with it. The notion seemed absurd, certainly nothing concrete on which to base it, but it persisted.

Something that bolstered the idea was the surprising, utterly unexpected appearance of the outlaw bunch that chased him and Mary Merril. They must have emerged from the lower brush only a short distance west of the north mouth of Echo Canyon. As he told the girl, it was highly illogical to believe that they had been holed up in the brush awaiting their appearance. That they were nowhere in evidence when he ascended the slope to the cliff top he was sure, for he had carefully scanned his surroundings before breasting the rise and had paused several times to examine the immediate terrain for as long as it was possible to view the rangeland. And from the crest of the slope there was a clear view in every direction.

Had they noted the girl making her way to the cliff top some time before he undertook the climb? That also seemed absurd. Had they designs on her they would have much more likely followed her up the slope. Definitely, that was out.

But blast it! They had to come from somewhere, again to all appearances, from the immediate neighborhood of Echo Canyon. They didn't emerge from the canyon, that was sure for certain; the row the echoes would have kicked up would have served ample warning of their approach. Slade swore under his breath from sheer exasperation. But the hunch persisted—somehow, Echo Canyon held the key to the mystery. How? He hadn't the slightest idea.

Common sense counselled that the logical thing to do was take a ride east along the base of the hills in the hope of spotting the hidden trail he must have overlooked. Anyhow, that would give him a chance to see.

He chuckled to himself as suddenly Sheriff Crane's remark rang in his ears—"You could do a lot worse." Maybe the sheriff hadn't been exactly talking through his hat. The little devil certainly had everything necessary to make a woman attractive and desirable. He began to wonder, perhaps with a certain disquietude, if this was *it*. Maybe he was caught in a loop he wouldn't be able to wriggle out of. And, to make matters worse, he was not exactly sure that he wanted to wriggle out.

The ancient allegory of Cupid and the arrows has never been improved upon: Cupid, who should never in the world have been trusted with a weapon, who defies all game laws, who shoots people in the bushes, the weak and the helpless and the strong and self-confident! There is no more reason in it than that. Walt Slade wondered if the little hellion had at last feathered a dart from his heart-shaped bow in *his* breast.

Well, at the moment he had something to think about other than curly dark hair, red lips, and big dark blue eues.

Incongruous as it might seem, another pair of blue eyes were also on his mind—the eyes of Juan Covelo, that at times looked like the eyes of a mad cat. His immediate chore was to run down Covelo and his bunch, and until that was accomplished, purely personal matters must be held in abeyance. He forced his straying thoughts to concentrate on the problem that confronted him.

Also, he was gravely concerned by the possibility—probability, rather—that Covelo was all set to pull something. Slade figured he still had at least a half dozen men left of his original bunch and an outlaw leader of his ability would have no trouble enlisting more, despite recent reversals.

But an outlaw leader must keep his followers well supplied with spending money did he hope to hold them in line. Before his, Slade's, arrival in the section, it appeared Covelo had enjoyed a very lucrative period; but the owlhoots let money slip through their fingers quickly and at the moment Covelo might well be scraping the bottom of his financial barrel. Which meant a replenishment of his exchequer was in order.

Where would he strike? That was a question to which Slade very much wished he had the answer. Could he just anticipate the outlaw's move, he might be able to thwart it. He hoped so, for if Covelo ran true to form, it was very likely that some innocent person or persons would die. The cold killer must be in anything but a charitable mood at present and would welcome a chance to vent his spleen on the first victim that crossed his path.

Which gave *El Halcón* cause for concern. He devoutly hoped that Covelo would make his next move against some unguarded herd. He evidently had a good market for wet cows and rustling operations could be carried on by a small band, with a minimum of risk. That might well be it; but there was no guarantee that it would be.

Sheriff Crane finished his snack and hurried back to his office, where he had work to do. Slade sat on a while over coffee and a cigarette. Draining his cup, he settled the score, waved to Hardrock Hogan and left the saloon, strolling along the main street until he reached a point from which he could see the splendor of the sunset flaming in the west.

Leaning against a convenient hitching post, he watched the chromatic display as the colors faded and softened to steel gray, to shadowy black, and the stars winked coyly at the answering stars that were the lights of Sanderson.

While the lovely blue dusk sifted down from the hilltops, he still stood where he was, smoking a cigarette and thinking deeply, but arriving at no satisfactory conclusion. He had a disquieting premonition that something unpleasant was due to happen. What? He had no idea, but the feeling persisted. Finally he pinched out the butt of his cigarette and returned to the Branding Pen, where he sat down and ordered coffee. Hardrock Hogan came over and dropped into a chair.

"Sorta quiet tonight," he remarked, glancing around. "Won't be tomorrow night, though. Tomorrow is payday for the railroaders and the boys will all be here, flush and whoppin' it up."

"Wouldn't be surprised," Slade agreed absently, for his thoughts were elsewhere.

After a few random remarks, Hardrock returned to the bar, leaving *El Halcón* to his coffee.

A little later, John Webb and Pancho Arista entered and joined Slade.

"Been over at Pancho's office, working, since late afternoon," the rancher announced. "Figure to run a double train south in the morning. Plenty of business in sight. Think you'll make it out to the spread tomorrow, son?"

"I hope to," Slade replied, "that is, if nothing happens."

However, something was going to happen that would nullify his plans.

17

WEBB AND Arista ordered a meal. Slade sat and talked with them while they consumed it. Then, feeling restless and ill at ease, he again left the saloon and headed for the sheriff's office, where he found Crane busy at his desk. He looked up inquiringly.

"Something on your mind?" he asked.

"I don't know, Tom," Slade replied, dropping into a chair and rolling a cigarette. "I've just got a feeling that something is going to happen."

"Another of your hunches, eh?" grunted Crane.

"Guess you might call it that," the Ranger conceded. "May be nothing but nervousness, but I've had a similar feeling before, and it usually worked out. Well, all we can do is wait and see."

"I'll try and get my paper work done before it busts loose," sighed the sheriff, scratching away with his pen.

He didn't.

Slade smoked and relaxed, busy with his thoughts. The pen scratched, the sheriff grumbled over his task. All was peaceful, for the moment.

Abruptly, outside sounded a shouting and a pound of feet on the board sidewalk. Into the office burst a wild-eyed man in greasy overalls. He held a long-spouted oil can which he waved frantically, and gasped for breath.

"They—they—they—" he stuttered.

"What in blazes is the matter with you, grease monkey?" roared the sheriff. "What the blankety-blank—"

Slade's voice cut in. "Easy, feller, catch your breath and tell us what's wrong," he said to the excited oiler.

Under the impact of that quiet voice and the steady eyes that regarded him, the grease monkey cooled down, caught his breath and spoke in a normal manner.

"The pay car," he said. "They robbed it—seven of 'em. The door was locked but they opened it somehow. The pay-

master and his clerk were making up the pay roll. They busted
'em over the head with pistol barrels and cleaned the safe."

"Either badly hurt?" Slade asked.

"Dunno for sure," replied the oiler. "The paymaster was
still unconscious when I left. Clerk wasn't hurt much, I
reckon; must have a thick skull. Had sense enough to lay low
on the floor and not move till they were gone. Otherwise I
reckon they'd have finished him off."

"Quite likely," Slade agreed. "Know which way they
went?"

The oiler shook his head. "Can't see the trail from the
part of the yard where the pay car is on a spur," he explained.

"And there were seven of them?"

"That's what the clerk said."

"Masked?"

"Clerk said they were, black masks all over their faces."

Slade stood up. "I slipped badly," he remarked bitterly to
Crane. "Hardrock Hogan told me tomorrow is payday for
the railroad, but I was thinking of something else and didn't
pay any attention to what he said, or its possible significance."

"A man can't think of everything," growled the sheriff.
"What you aim to do?"

"I'm going to play still another hunch," Slade replied.
"Round up your deputies fast as you can."

"I think they're all three over at the Regan House playing
cards, that's where they were headed for when they left
here, a little while ago," said Crane. "Pete," he ordered the
grease monkey, "hightail over there and tell 'em to grab
their crowbaits and meet us here at the office."

"Certain," replied the oiler and departed with haste.

"Which way we riding, Walt?" the sheriff asked as they
hurried to the stable where their mounts were stalled.

"East," Slade replied.

"You figure they went east?"

"I do."

After which the sheriff held his peace, knowing that *El
Halcón* would reveal his plans when he saw fit, and not before.

Shortly after they returned to the office, the three deputies
charged up, ready to go.

Slade set the pace, and it was a fast one. It would have
been faster only he had to curb Shadow in deference to the
other horses.

Finally the sheriff could contain himself no longer. "Walt,
where you headed for, tell me, won't you?" he begged.

"Echo Canyon," the Ranger replied.

"You figure they'll go through the canyon?"

"They won't," Slade stated decisively. "They have their own way by which they cross the hills, wherever that is, but I believe by making speed and going through Echo Canyon we may be able to intercept them. Undoubtedly where they hit the rangeland is not far from the north mouth of the canyon. My opinion is that they will head for the northern hills where quite likely they have some sort of a hole-up where they can lie snug for a while. At least that's the hunch I'm following. If I'm wrong, we won't have lost anything except a little sleep."

"And if you happen to be right, we may get a chance to bag the sidewinders," said Crane. "I figure it's worth giving a try."

As they rode, Slade constantly scanned the terrain ahead, although he thought there was little likelihood that the outlaws would pause before reaching their secret way across the hills. Nor did he believe there was much chance the posse would overtake them before they turned from the trail. Due to confusion and uncertainty in the railroad yards nearly an hour had elapsed from the time of the robbery till the sheriff's office was notified. He did believe, however, that the crossing of the hills would be a much longer route than the straight shoot through Echo Canyon.

And he thought it unlikely that the bunch would follow the trail through the canyon, for various reasons, one being that the echoes would herald their approach to anyone who might be out on the range or headed for town. The canyon route was used by several of the spreads to the north and east and there was no telling when a band of cowhands on their way to Sanderson might be utilizing the short cut to the railroad town.

Drawing near the canyon, Slade slowed the pace somewhat. For although Shadow showed no indications of distress, the other horses were blowing a little and he did not wish to have them winded when they passed through the gorge.

Hopefully, he scanned the slopes to the north, in the chance that the outlaws might provide evidence that they were negotiating the crossing. Even the faint flicker of a lighted match touched to a cigarette would not escape his gaze.

But the hills remained silent and deserted, with no sign of human life. Occasionally an owl would drift by on silent wings, or a night hawk scream in passing. Otherwise the night was deathly still, a tomb of silence under the swung censers of the stars.

They reached the canyon, entered it. Slade became even more vigilant, for did anybody else happen to be in the gorge, they would quickly be notified of the posse's presence.

The whisper, murmur, mutter of the echoes began; soon they were going at full blast. Slade swore as the din assailed his ears. Echoes are delightful and romantic things, but he'd had more than enough of them in that infernal hole.

Accompanied by the chorus of booming and bellowing, they bulged from the north mouth of the canyon. Slade swept the prairie with his gaze. Fully a thousand yards to the east and north, seven horsemen were sweeping across the range, heading east by slightly north.

"There they go!" he shouted. "Sift sand, boys, sift sand!"

The posse responded, and the chase was on. The horses also responded, seeming to catch the spirit of the race. They snorted, slugged their heads above the bits and poured their bodies over the ground.

The outlaws were well-mounted, but so was the posse. Slowly, slowly, but steadily the distance that separated the two bands decreased. The thousand yards shrank to nine hundred, to eight, and still the quarry held to the course, east by slightly north, apparently with a definite objective in view. Slade wondered where the hellions were headed for.

Then as the robber band veered more to the north, abruptly he understood.

The canyon that provided sanctuary for him and Mary Merril the night before! Let the devils reach that stony labyrinth and they would be safe from pursuit. There would be no rooting them out of that tangled maze of canyons and cracks and gorges and gulleys, with which they were doubtless familiar. Even were they not, the advantage would be with them. They could slide into any opening they chose, and trying to figure out which would be the purest guesswork, with the ever present hazard that they might hole up and wait to blow the pursuers from under their hats. And now the canyon mouth was close to where they rode.

With a disgusted oath he slid his Winchester from the boot; his voice rang out, "Trail, Shadow, trail!"

Instantly the great black extended himself, pulling away from the other horses as if they were standing still. The amazed and protesting shouts of his companions rang in his ears. Slade estimated the distance—less than six hundred yards, now. A little more and he would be close enough, even in the vague starlight.

Evidently the outlaws figured he was already too blasted

close. From their ranks flame flickered. Slugs whined past, none of them too close, so far. But they quickly came closer, uncomfortably close.

Still Slade held his fire, estimating the distance to the canyon mouth. Blast it, he'd have to risk it! His voice sounded again, "Steady, Shadow!"

The horse leveled off to his smooth running-walk. Slade clamped the rifle to his shoulder, his eyes glanced along the sights.

The muzzle spouted fire. One of the riders pitched sideways from the saddle to lie motionless. Slade fired again. A second man lurched, swayed, grabbed the saddle horn, but kept his seat.

But now the remaining owlhoots were in the shadow. Slade emptied the magazine in their direction with little hope of scoring a hit. Behind him his companions' rifles were banging away, with no results. Another moment and the robber band had vanished into the black mouth of the canyon.

"Ease off, feller," Slade said, and pulled Shadow to a halt. He was reloading his rifle when the posse surged up to him.

"Ain't we going in after them?" yelled the sheriff, blazing with excitement.

"We are not," Slade stated flatly. "I know that hole. They're in the clear, and that's all there is to it."

The posse swore wholeheartedly but didn't argue the point.

"Anyhow, you got one of the skunks," said Crane, gesturing to the still form on the ground a little farther ahead.

"Yes, but I'll wager it isn't Covelo," Slade replied bitterly. "I really *am* beginning to believe the hellion bears a charmed life. Seems he always gets the breaks, in one way or another. Well, he has his stake. That pay car must have been loaded. It meets pay rolls at Alpine and El Paso, as well as at Sanderson. Yes, he's set up in business again, for a while."

Crane growled profane assent.

"Catch that cayuse and load the carcass onto it," he told the deputies, waving his hand toward the dead outlaw's horse which had run but a short distance before halting.

The dead man was not masked, that article being discovered in his saddle pouches.

"Guess they figured they wouldn't need them after they cleared Sanderson," Slade decided. "Imagine they are not overly comfortable to wear."

"Mean-lookin' cuss," grunted the sheriff. "Anybody remember seeing him before?"

Nobody did.

On the chance that he might unearth some of the pay car money, Crane hopefully rummaged the saddle pouches, but found nothing of significance.

"Chances are Covelo carried all or most of the money," Slade remarked. "Guess we might as well amble home; done all we can for tonight."

"Could have been worse," Crane replied cheerfully. "For a while, with lead whistling all around you, I was scairt things weren't going to end up so good. I'd say you and *amigo* Covelo have something in common—looks like you both bear charmed lives. Okay, boys, all set? Let's go."

During the ride to Sanderson the sheriff and deputies chattered away, conning over the night's happenings, but Slade had little to say. He was busy puzzling over how in blazes the outlaws managed to cross the hills so quickly. He had been confident that they would not put in an appearance until after the posse debouched from Echo Canyon.

———— 18

PROGRESS WAS slow on the return trip and it was full day when they reached Sanderson. Pretty well worn out, Slade tumbled into bed and slept soundly until past noon. After breakfasting he repaired to the sheriff's office to learn more details concerning the robbery.

"Devils did all right by themselves," Crane told him. "Got away with between thirty-five and forty thousand dollars. Oh, they worked it smooth, all right. Paymaster swears the door was locked, that they must have had a duplicate key."

"Or, if he left the key in the lock, used a pair of long-jawed pliers," Slade commented. "Among his other questionable talents, Covelo is an expert cracksman. I doubt if there's a safe anywhere around he can't open. Didn't they have a guard keeping an eye on the pay car?"

"Yep, they had a guard," the sheriff replied. "They found him later, alongside the car with his head busted open. Doc is afraid he may have a concussion of the brain. Got his senses back this morning and told what happened. They worked that one slick. He said the feller who banged him over the head was dressed like a yard switchman and even carried a lantern. Reckon he carried a gun in the other hand he held behind him. Said they were going to switch the pay car to another siding. Watchman looked the direction he pointed and he slammed him one. That's all he remembered till the doctor asked him how he felt. Oh, they worked it slick, all right."

"Covelo usually does," Slade commented.

"So I reckon with a good stake in his jeans, he'll lie low for a while, eh?"

Slade did not immediately answer but sat smoking thoughtfully, while the sheriff watched him in silence and expectation. *El Halcón* was, in fact, reliving his experiences on the trail of Juan Covelo since he first contacted the outlaw leader in El Paso County, unmasked his disguise, and learned his true identity. Finally he spoke.

"I'm not so sure he'll refrain from activity," he said. "That is what it is logical to believe he'll do, as any average owlhoot would do, with him and his bunch going on a spending spree somewhere to celebrate their success. But I have learned from bitter experience that with Covelo there is one thing to be depended upon."

"What's that?" asked Crane.

"That he will do the unexpected," Slade replied. "I wouldn't be at all surprised if he pulls something else immediately, figuring that we will be confident he won't. That's the way he works, and it may give us a chance to outguess him, something we haven't been very successful at so far."

"Wouldn't say that," differed the sheriff. "I figure you did a pretty good chore of outguessing him several times. The raid on Pancho Arista's cart train, for one, busting up his try at widelooping John Webb's cows for another. To say nothing of handing him the works when he tried to drygulch you and me on the way to Marathon. And you must have given him a hell of a scare last night."

Slade chuckled. "You make out a pretty good case for me," he conceded. "But the fact remains that Covelo is still running loose and capable of raising the devil some more."

"Yep, but I figure his rope is getting mighty, mighty short and will soon be short enough to choke him," Crane predicted confidentially.

"Hope you're right," Slade smiled. "Well, we'll see."

Crane glanced at his watch. "Cooper insists on holding an inquest on that carcass nobody recognizes, so I reckon we'd better amble over to his office," he said. "What you figure to do afterward?"

"Haven't made up my mind yet," Slade replied. "Getting rather late."

"Take it easy today, for a change," advised the sheriff. "More money is being rushed to Sanderson and the railroad boys will have their bust tonight, after all. Some of the spreads are paying off today, too, and things should be lively."

"Sounds interesting," Slade admitted. "Well, let's go and listen to the coroner's jury say that scalawag got what was coming to him and advise you to run down the rest of the bunch in a hurry."

Crane swore disgustedly and was still mumbling under his breath when they left the office.

Slade was relieved to learn from Doc Cooper that neither the paymaster nor the car guard had suffered permanent damage. The clerk, who received a glancing blow and had sense enough to play 'possum until the robbers were gone, was already up and around.

"At least the hellions didn't kill anybody this time," growled Crane.

"But not from any kindly motive," Slade said. "They just preferred not to chance making a racket and rousing the yards—railroad police around there. A quick blow on the head was silent, and effective enough for their purpose."

A little later one of the railroad police visited the office, eager to hear the details of the chase and the killing of one outlaw. He shook his bristly head when the tale was finished.

"You know the blankety-blank who runs the bunch?" he asked of Slade.

"I have contacted him," the Ranger replied, an amused gleam in his eyes, for he guessed what was running through the other's mind.

"Well, all I've got to say is that I'd like to meet up with the devil," the policeman declared.

"I certainly hope you don't," Slade said.

"Why not?" the other demanded, a little truculently.

Slade let the full force of his pale eyes rest on the other's face.

"Because," he said quietly, "you would die."

The railroad man looked a bit startled.

"Is he really that bad?" he asked.

"I doubt if there are more than a few men, if any, who can shade him with a gun," Slade answered, adding, "Of course he might prefer to take you alive, peg you out over an ant hill so the ants could polish your bones after they had finished with the rest of you. Or tie you on top of a cliff where the vultures nest, slash your face, and leave you for them to peck out your eyes and tear open your throat. He has done just that to others."

The policeman shivered. "You can have him!" he declared, and departed in haste.

"Well, you threw a scare into that jigger," chuckled Crane. "Why did you do it?"

"Overconfidence can sometimes get one into serious trouble," Slade explained. "Not that there's much danger of him contacting Covelo, but you can't always tell."

The afternoon wore on, a globe of light and fragrance. The never-ceasing marvel of the sunset flung its shattered rainbow across the sky. Sanderson's canyon wall glowed with orange flame that dulled and vanished under the sifting blue dust of the dusk. Night brooded over the rangeland like a nesting bird.

Sanderson's habitual busy hum quickened, developed a shriller note that got louder as the hours of darkness passed. The railroaders had received their pay and all save those who worked the night shift were busy celebrating in the various saloons, including the Branding Pen, ably assisted by the cowhands from several spreads that had also paid off, and by gentlemen and ladies of doubtful antecedents who were always to be found in the canyon town.

The Branding Pen was packed. Men at the bar reached over the shoulders of other men to have their glasses refilled. The games were going full blast, the dance-floor was crowded. The smoky air quivered to the babble of conversation. The gathering was boisterous but fairly orderly and Hardrock Hogan and his floor men had no trouble keeping things under control.

Walt Slade enjoyed it for a while, but around midnight, growing weary of the continual racket and feeling there was little chance of any serious trouble developing, went to bed.

Meanwhile grim drama was taking place on the Triangle Dot range just east of John Webb's Cross W holding.

The Triangle Dot was not a big spread but raised good stock. The nucleus of a trail herd, about a hundred head, was gathered on the banks of a little stream that wound through a scattering of big trees. A single night hawk rode around the small herd, singing in a voice that could have been improved upon. The cows, however, perhaps being slightly tone deaf, seemed to find the sound soothing.

The night hawk ambled along under the low-lying branches of one of the trees, following his accustomed route. From above a tight loop snaked down, settled over his head and shoulders, and was instantly jerked taut, hurling him to the ground with stunning force. From the tree dropped a man who ran to the prostrate puncher, who was writhing and kicking and striving to rise. A gun barrel crunched against his skull and he went limp.

A second man dropped from the tree, flipped loose his rope and coiled it. Both turned and waved their hands.

From a thicket a few hundred yards distant rode four more men, the hair of one gleaming golden in the bright starlight. They led two saddled and bridled horses.

Very quickly the herd was started moving, heading south by west.

At that very moment the night hawk's relief was approaching from the Triangle Dot ranchhouse, only a couple of miles distant, and saw the herd vanishing into the southeast. He sped to the feeding ground and discovered the fallen night hawk, his horse standing patiently a few yards distant. He managed to load the unconscious form onto the saddle, roped it in place, and set out for the ranchhouse.

The Triangle Dot hands mounted in hot haste and set off in pursuit of the widelooped cows. Then, as Ralph Logan, the Triangle Dot range boss, told it to Sheriff Crane and Walt Slade early the following afternoon, "We couldn't have been much more'n a mile behind those blasted sidewinders when we sighted the south hills near Echo Canyon. But we didn't sight no cows. We figured they run 'em into Echo Canyon, so we hightailed through that noisy hole. But when we came out the south mouth to where we could see for miles in every direction, there still weren't no cows in sight. We nosed around the brush for a while but couldn't find hide or hair of 'em. Where in blazes they went I don't know!"

"Then what did you do?" asked the sheriff.

"The only sensible thing to do," grunted Logan. "We went home to bed. The Old Man figured I'd better ride to town and tell you what happened, so I did. But what I'd like to know is where in the blinkin' blue blazes did those critters go?"

The sheriff turned to Slade. "Where do you think they went, Walt?" he asked.

"Across the Rio Grande to where somebody doubtless was waiting to receive them," Slade replied laconically.

Logan stared at him. "But, blast it! They couldn't have kept on goin' south without us spottin' them," he protested.

"If you'd hung around the canyon mouth for an hour or two, you might have," Slade returned. "They were not moved on south until the coast was clear."

"You mean to say they weren't shoved through the canyon?"

"They were not," Slade stated. "They were shoved across the hills by some route known only to the rustlers. Known only to them for the time being, at least," he added grimly with a significance that was lost on the range boss.

"Reckon you must be right," sighed Logan. "That is, unless they sprouted wings."

"Highly unlikely, I'd say," Slade replied, with a smile. "Thank you, Logan, for bringing the sheriff word of what was done; it may be of help."

"I hope so," said Logan. "Looks like nothing or nobody is safe hereabouts any more. Well, I'm going to get me a snort. I need it."

"Was the night hawk badly injured?" Slade asked.

"Nothing to bother about," returned Logan. "Sore head, but that's all. He's out on the job."

After the range boss departed, Crane turned questioningly to Slade.

"I'm riding to the Cross W ranchhouse," the Ranger said. "Aim to get an early start tomorrow morning and try again to find that hidden way through the hills."

"You were right about Covelo pulling something in a hurry," Crane commented.

"Yes, he works fast, as I expected he would," Slade agreed. "But he may have made a slip that will prove costly for him. He has narrowed my search. If Logan had his facts straight, and I think he did, the way through the hills must be very close to Echo Canyon. Otherwise the herd would still have been in sight as they approached the canyon. Well, we'll see."

——— 19

Slade wasted no time getting the rig on Shadow, for the afternoon was passing and he hoped to reach the Cross W ranchhouse before dark. At the north mouth of Echo Canyon he pulled to a halt and for several minutes sat gazing along the base of the brush-grown hills, already hazy in the shadows of approaching night, the concentration furrow deep between his black brows.

"Horse, I'm getting a notion," he told his mount. "A sorta loco notion, it would seem, but that sort has worked out before. I've been wondering for quite a while what causes those unusual echoes, and I believe I've hit on it. Somehow all along I've had the hazy feeling that rackety hole held the key to the mystery. Well, come daylight tomorrow and we'll give my theory a workout. Never mind scoffing, you may have to eat your words."

He wished he could reach the western cliff crests; what he would be able to see from the elevation might provide a clue that would simplify matters.

But for some distance west of the canyon, the slopes could not be climbed. With a final glance around he rode on, heavy with thought.

It was dark when he reached the Cross W ranchhouse, but the warmth of the welcome he received left nothing to be desired.

"Well, son," remarked old John, as they sat in the living room after supper, smoking and talking, "have you been thinking over the proposition I made you?"

"Yes, I've been thinking on it, seriously," Slade replied.

"But haven't reached a decision, yet?"

"That's so," Slade admitted.

"Well, I hope you decide the right way," said Webb. "Somebody else hopes so, too," he added with a significant glance at Mary Merril, who smiled and blushed.

"There are certainly reasons why I should consider it very seriously," the Ranger answered, his eyes on Mary's face. Old John chuckled. Mary lowered her dark lashes.

After old John had gone to bed, Mary was silent for some minutes, while Slade smoked and watched her. Abruptly she raised her eyes to meet his squarely.

"Walt," she said, "I think I can understand why you hesitate to accept Uncle John's offer. I think I have known it all along."

"Yes, I think you have," Slade agreed soberly. "Because of which you can understand why it is difficult for me to reach a decision. Unfortunately, one cannot always give way to one's desires. Yes, I think you have guessed quite accurately, but I also think you have a right to know for sure."

From a cunningly concealed secret pocket in his broad leather belt he drew something that he handed to her. For a long and silent moment she gazed at the famous silver star set on a silver circle, the feared and honored badge of the Texas Rangers. With a deep sigh, she handed it back to him.

"Yes, as I guessed," she said. "And old Miguel was right —you heed the call of duty, a tie that is hard to break, and it is a lonely trail, a lonely trail. But perhaps—" she left the sentence unfinished. He finished it for her.

"Yes, a lonely trail, but trails have a habit of bending back on themselves, and there is always the chance that one may *turn* back, if the pull is strong enough."

For another moment she was silent. Then her mood changed. She shot him a laughing glance.

"Today is ours," she said softly. "We'll make the most of it." With a graceful gesture she extinguished the light.

The following morning, his face shining with pleasant memories, Walt Slade rode south by west. He rode steadily until he reached the mouth of Echo Canyon. Here he drew rein and sat studying the cracked and fissured west wall. The cliffs were limestone and highly vulnerable to the erosive effects of wind and rain. Doubtless the fissures and rents had been hollowed out by recurrent freezes and thaws during the course of thousands of years.

Finally he urged Shadow on and rode west very slowly, hugging the brush that encroached on the level rangeland, his eyes surveying every inch of the thorny tangle.

He had covered less than two hundred feet of slow going when he pulled to a halt once more, his eyes glowing with triumph.

"Here it is, horse, just as I finally expected," he said. "An old trick, but it works."

Only the keenest vision could have noticed the slight change in the appearance of the chaparral wall. For perhaps eight or ten feet, the leaves were slightly shrivelled and grayed, with here and there a dangling twig that had been almost severed from the parent bough.

He dismounted, walked to the growth, stooped down, and seized one of the slender trunks and heaved.

The trunk came out of the ground easily, for it was rootless, the roots replaced by a sharpened end, much like that of a stake. He laid the bush aside and tackled another, and yet another. Soon he had an opening in the leafy wall wide enough for Shadow to squeeze through. Beyond, the growth had been cut away providing a narrow corridor to the face of the cliff only a few feet distant.

And in the beetling face was a dark opening, the mouth of a cave.

"Yep, this is how they did it," he told Shadow. "Cut away the brush to make a passage to the cave mouth, which Covelo, who seems to know everything, somehow found out about. The outer bushes were replaced after the cows were driven in, and a casual observer riding but a few yards from the base of the cliff would never suspect anything of that sort. And I'll wager a hatful of pesos that the cave runs right on through to the south slope of the hills. Well, we'll soon see about that. And perhaps I'll be able to learn what I still don't know—what causes that unusual echo in the outer canyon. Just a minute, horse. I see some stands of sotol over to the right, and dry sotol stalks make good torches. Looks dark inside that hole, but what do you want to bet we'll lack for light once we're well inside? Bet you we won't."

Breaking off several of the dry stalks, he laid them aside. Next, with the greatest care, he replaced the cut bushes. After which he gathered up the stalks, mounted, and struck a match to one; it burned with a clear flame.

"In you go," he told Shadow, whose hoofbeats rang hollow as they entered the cave. Almost immediately the bore turned sharply to the left, continued for perhaps a hundred feet, then curved to the south. And there was light, light flowing through the fissures in the rock wall to the east. Slade saw that the tunnel was not more than a score of feet in width.

It was a weird place. Here and there from the rock floor

rose grotesquely sculped stalagmites, with similar stalactites, like big icicles, suspended from the distant roof of the bore.

"Formed by the drip of calcareous water depositing calcium carbonate during an epoch of time," he explained to Shadow. "A formation not at all unusual in limestone caves."

Another moment and he let out a low whistle. "But ahead *is* something unusual," he said. "I never before saw or heard of anything quite like it."

Rising from the cave floor, just about bisecting the width of the tunnel, was a very thin wall of rock that soared upward almost to the lofty roof. Not more than four feet wide at the base, it narrowed to a knife-edge at its crest. Light pouring through the fissures in the cave wall to the east glittered on the myriad facets of its shattered surface, facets that seemed held together by magic, each fragment threatening to fall.

It was nothing more than an amazingly extended stalagmite continuing into the distance of the bore.

And the mystery of Echo Canyon was no longer a mystery. The thin and broken wall was just a gigantic sounding board that vibrated to sounds concentrated by the openings in the canyon wall and magnified them a hundredfold.

"Very simple, like Columbus standing the egg on end, once you see it," Slade remarked to Shadow. "Okay, horse, let's move on. I only hope that blasted thing doesn't take a notion to tumble down on our heads; looks like it would do so any minute."

It was a shivery passage. The beat of Shadow's irons brought eerie rumblings and whisperings from the wall that were hard on the nerves. Shadow snorted his apprehension and disgust and planted each forward-reaching hoof gingerly, although the smoothness of the rock floor was broken only by an occasional small stalagmite or some slight fall of rift.

Very quickly, however, Slade was heartened by the indubitable evidence that cattle and horses had passed that way shortly before.

"Yes, they ran the Triangle Dot herd through here, all right," he remarked to his mount. "This may work out all to the good for us. How? Right now I haven't the slightest notion, but we'll work it out somehow. At least we're not blundering around in the dark any more, not knowing which way to turn. With definite knowledge how they do it now, it's just up to us to take advantage of what we've learned. We'll do so, horse, somehow."

He continued on his way, discovering no pitfalls, no

obstructions. He surmised that the length of the cavern would be something less than that of the outer canyon and that it would continue to parallel the course of the gorge.

The explanation of how it came to be was, Slade knew, geologically simple. Once upon a time a vast amount of water had flowed this way, hollowing out the gorge that was Echo Canyon and, seeking a path of least resistance, forcing its way through the broken and soluble limestone formation and eventually producing the cave. Of course there might have been other factors involved, such as subsidence or elevation due to distant volcanic disturbances. Even so, the Chisos Mountains, also a limestone-based formation, had been raised from the level floor of the southwest wastelands. Just another example of the slow, resistless forces of nature working through untold ages to provide something that in due time man would turn to his own uses, good or bad.

He must be, Slade felt sure, nearing the south mouth of the passage. The bore was widening considerably and evidently the arm of the cave beyond the wall must be narrowing in consequence, perhaps blocked altogether. Very probably so, he believed.

All things must come to an end and abruptly the unusual sounding board ceased to be, cut off short as by a gigantic knife. And here it appeared thinner and more broken and more ominous than farther north. He was heartily glad to get from beneath its threat. And only a few yards farther on was the south mouth of the cave.

It opened into a little cup barely a hundred feet in diameter. Directly opposite was a steep slope up which the semblance of a trail ran several hundred yards to a sharp crest.

After a glance around, Slade rode on across the cup and tackled the slope. Pushing cows up the steep sag would be a chore, but it evidently could be done, for plain to see were the signs of their passage.

Shadow expressed his dissatisfaction vocally as he breasted the rise. However, he did not pause until, blowing a bit, he reached the crest, where Slade reined him in for a breather.

From his point of vantage, he could see for miles across the open land; the spot provided a perfect watch tower.

The far slope was not nearly so steep and the trail, a mere trace, continued down it, through a hazy green tunnel roofed and hidden from view by interlacing foliage.

For a while, Slade sat smoking a cigarette and gazing across the far distances, until Shadow had caught his breath. Then he once more continued on his way, reaching the level ground without incident. He rode on for a short distance, turned and gazed back at the way he had come. There was nothing to show that what he had passed through existed. It was a perfect crossing for purloined cattle. He carefully noted his position in relation to certain landmarks, so that he would have no difficulty in spotting the hidden track and rode on until he reached the east-west trail. Then he headed for Sanderson, highly elated over what he had learned, although to just what use to put the knowledge he at the moment had no idea.

Reaching the canyon town, he stabled his horse, had a bite to eat, and then repaired to the sheriff's office to give Crane an account of his experiences.

The sheriff voiced profane amazement as the tale unfolded. "So that's how the hellions do it!" he exclaimed. "I never heard the like."

"Nothing particularly outstanding about such a formation in a limestone region," Slade explained. "That is, other than that stalagmite sounding board, which is strange and contrary to experience, although admitting of quite a simple explanation. A crack in the cave roof through which there was a steady drip of calcareous water. The wall it built up would naturally be narrow at the base and grow still narrower as the barrier rose. A process that took untold time, but nature is never in a hurry and what she finally accomplishes is amazing, from our viewpoint. Once in an Arizona cave I saw a stalagmite shaped exactly like a pulpit, and it must have weighed a hundred tons. All constructed by countless little drops of falling water.

"The cave is a bit shorter than the canyon; that's why there are no echoes in the south end of the gorge. The Indians knew of all those cracks through the hills and put them to use—I've encountered similar conditions before—and somehow Covelo learned of that particular one. Perhaps from some old trapper, hunter, or prospector. Those desert rats prowled the hills and, like the Indians, learned all their secrets. Anyhow, he learned about it and saw its possibilities; he never misses a bet."

" 'Pears somebody else I could mention never misses one, either," commented Crane. Slade laughed and changed the subject.

"Masking the passage through the chaparral to the cave mouth with the cut brush is an old trick," he resumed. "However, he got a mite careless and failed to replace the growth with fresh bushes once the leaves began to wither. That was the give-away. Right from the beginning I had a vague feeling that the canyon and those echoes were tied up somehow with the way through the hills, but it took me quite a while to figure it. I was concentrating on a trail up the slope and that sorta washed the other angle out of my mind. But the night they chased Mary Merril and myself I got to wondering where in blazes they came from. Then the night of the pay car robbery they again made their appearance apparently from nowhere. Right then I was convinced they didn't reach the rangeland by way of a trail over the hills. So if they didn't go over them, they must go through them. The rest was simple."

"Uh-huh, very simple, only everybody else, including myself, was too darn simple to think of it," Crane said dryly. "And now you know how they do it, what's the next move?"

"Frankly, I don't know, yet," Slade admitted. "Anyhow, tomorrow I'm going to ride down there and have a look at that hole and its approaches from this side. Maybe I can think of something."

"A bad place to be prowling around in by yourself," demurred the sheriff. "Get caught by a rock fall in there and you'd starve to death before somebody managed to locate that hole and root you out."

"Oh, those rocks have been hanging there for a million years or so, and I imagine they'll stand for a while longer, unless something happens to bring them down," Slade returned carelessly.

The sheriff grunted, and did not look entirely satisfied.

"Everything quiet hereabouts?" Slade asked.

"Yep, so far," Crane replied. "Getting a little breathing spell for a change, it 'pears. Which is welcome. A day without anything bad happening is a plumb novelty. Arista started another cart train moving this morning and he said Webb will be in tomorrow with some offers for new business. They're going to make a go of it, thanks to you."

Slade took it easy the rest of the day, went to bed fairly early and enjoyed a good night's sleep. After breakfast the following morning he got the rig on Shadow and rode east.

It was another beautiful day and he did not push Shadow who appeared content to amble along at a fair pace. Reaching the vicinity of the secret trail, Slade mounted the crest of the long slope and sat for a while surveying his surroundings. Satisfied that everything was in order, he sent Shadow down the opposite side to the cup, crossed it and entered the cave.

He had just reached the beginning of the stalagmite sounding board when his keen ears caught a sound, the sound of horses approaching from the north, and close.

Instantly his mind worked at hair-trigger speed. What the devil to do! If he turned and rode out of the cave, he could not hope to reach the crest of the steep sag before the approaching outlaws spotted him. The west arm of the cave was here but a narrow fissure into which he could not squeeze. And already he could hear the voices of the nearing horsemen. He was neatly trapped!

Just one thing to do—stand and shoot it out with the devils, with the odds five or six to one. And he must give them a chance to surrender before opening fire.

Whipping from the saddle, he forced Shadow against the far wall of the cave and took up his post at the edge of the stalagmite sounding board, guns ready. Here the cave was a bit gloomier than farther to the north, which might work to his advantage.

Into view came the riders, six in number. A shaft of light gleamed on Juan Covelo's yellow hair. Slade's voice rang out. "Elevate! You're covered! In the name of the state of Texas—"

A storm of exclamations drowned the rest of the command. Covelo swerved his horse sideways, whipping out his gun in the same move. Slade snapped a shot at him, but the light was poor, Covelo on the move. Another instant and he was behind his companions. The cave boomed and thundered to the bellow of gunfire.

Shooting with both hands, Slade saw a man whirl from his saddle, another topple sideways. Answering slugs stormed past him, showering him with fragments chipped from the stone. His left sleeve was in ribbons, blood trickling from a bullet-grazed arm. Another slug turned his hat sideways on his head. The odds were too great—there could be but one end to the uneven battle. He strove to get another shot at Covelo before he was downed. The hammers of his guns clicked on empty shells.

—— 20

SUDDENLY THE crackle of reports was drowned by a mighty roar. He saw Covelo whirl his horse even as a vast shadow swooped down and blotted out all things. It was followed by an earth-shaking crash. A section of the sounding board wall had fallen.

Dazed, numb, Slade reeled back and back to escape the flying fragments. Dimly he heard a mighty rumbling running slowly up the cave. The whole wall was coming down!

The rumbling roar lessened, died to a mutter, ceased altogether. A deathly silence shrouded the cave.

Lurching, staggering, still half dazed, Slade stumbled to where Shadow, trembling with fright, stood where he had been left. He leaned against the horse's shoulder, stroking its neck, talking to it in soothing tones until its fear subsided.

"The vibrations set up by the gunfire were all that was needed to give those hanging rocks a final push," he muttered. "A lucky break for me, though, feller. I sure figured it was curtains. Would have been in another second if that hadn't happened."

Automatically he reloaded his guns and holstered them. He walked to where the mass of fragments rose much higher than his head. Still a bit numb, he wondered vaguely if Juan Covelo lay there, crushed under a million tons of stone, or had he been able to keep ahead of the slowly falling wall and escape.

He didn't know. Perhaps he would never know.

Returning to Shadow, he mounted and rode out of the grim cave of death. Never had the warm sunshine been so welcome. Without looking back, he crossed the cup and ascended the steep slope, very slowly. On the crest of the rise he drew rein and sat motionless for some time, trying to banish from his ears a sound he had heard the instant after the wall crashed down—a whimpering squeal like the agonized plaint of a stepped-on rat.

Still riding slowly, he descended the far sag to the level land and headed for Echo Canyon. Reaching the gorge he turned into it and, slowing his mount a little more, rode north.

But now no booming echoes greeted his ears. Only the click of Shadow's irons broke the utter silence.

Echo Canyon was no more!

Soon it would be but legend, a figment of some old-timer's imagination. And another generation would not believe it ever existed.

At the north mouth of the canyon he turned west and rode parallel to the base of the cliffs. A few minutes later, he drew rein and sat gazing at the gaping opening in the wall of chaparral. Several of the cut bushes lay scattered about. Somebody had managed to escape the falling wall and get in the clear. Covelo? Possibly. But then again, possibly not. There was no way to tell. The rangeland lay lonely and deserted, bathed in the golden sunshine. The grim hills to the north kept their secret well.

Riding on till he came to a trickle of water, Slade removed the rig and allowed Shadow to drink and graze while he stretched out in the sunshine and smoked. He still felt a bit numb from the horror he had witnessed. To pass out swiftly and cleanly by way of a bullet was one thing, but to lie trapped and crushed beneath the stone, doomed to a lingering death by starvation and thirst was something different. Which was what might have happened to one or more of the outlaws. He still couldn't banish that awful whimpering squeal.

Gradually his mood lightened. After all things hadn't worked out too bad. For even if Covelo were not dead, he was convinced that the Sanderson section would not be troubled anymore by the outlaw and his bunch. Which was something accomplished. He rolled another cigarette and relaxed in a more comfortable frame of mind.

Finally he pinched out the butt, glanced at the westering sun and stood up.

"Feller, I'm going to have one more look into that infernal hole, just in case," he told Shadow. "You stay here and take it easy."

He entered the cave on foot, groping his way along through the darkness until he came to where light poured through the fissures in the canyon wall. There he paused.

Before him rose the same pitiless mound of stone. As he suspected, the stalagmite sounding board had collapsed from end to end. For several minutes he stood and gazed, then retraced his way to the open air.

With a glance at the westering sun, he replaced the rig and rode east, turning into Echo Canyon.

"Guess we'd better amble to Sanderson and inform Sheriff Crane of what happened," he decided.

Shadow offered no objections, so he rode on steadily, reaching the canyon town well after dark.

"I told you you had no business prowling around down there by yourself," Sheriff Crane scolded when the story of the final episode with the Covelo bunch was ended. "It's a plumb wonder you didn't get your comeuppance."

"I didn't, so that's all that counts," Slade replied cheerfully.

"Also I've a prime notion that you stopped some other devilment they had planned," Crane added. "Otherwise, why should they have been heading south like they were? Yep, they had something in mind, and it wouldn't have been nice, I'll bet a hatful of pesos on that.

"And you figure your chore here is finished?"

"Yes," Slade said. "Even if Covelo did manage to get in the clear, I'm sure you won't be bothered with him anymore."

"And now?"

"Now I figure to amble over to the Cross W in the morning and visit with the folks there for a couple of days and then head for the post to see what else Captain Jim has lined up for me," Slade answered.

"And if you'll take my advice, you'll amble back here soon and settle down permanent," the sheriff counselled. "You've done enough."

"You may have something there," Slade conceded.

But even as he spoke, his eyes seemed to look off into the far distance, to the ever-advancing horizon, and the trail.

Three days later, Mary Merril watched him ride away, tall and graceful atop his great black horse, heading to where duty called.

She turned and walked slowly back to the ranchhouse, her shapely head bowed, her lips moving as if in prayer.

"A lonely trail," she murmured. "But sometimes a trail *does* turn."

THE END